If You See Me, Don't Say Hi

NEEL PATEL

If You See Me, Don't Say Hi

FLATIRON
BOOKS
NEW YORK

This is a work of fiction. All of the characters, organizations, and events portrayed in these stories are either products of the author's imagination or are used fictitiously.

The following stories have been previously published and may appear in a slightly different form in this book:

"Just a Friend," *Hyphen* (April 2017)

"The Taj Mahal," *Indiana Review* (volume 39, issue 1, summer 2017)

"These Things Happen," *American Literary Review* (fall 2015)

"An Arrangement," *The Southampton Review* (winter/spring 2016)

www.flatironbooks.com

Library of Congress Cataloging-in-Publication Data

Names: Patel, Neel author.
Title: If you see me, don't say hi : stories / Neel Patel.
Description: First edition. | New York : FLATIRON BOOKS, 2018.
Identifiers: LCCN 2018001437 | ISBN 9781250183194 (hardcover) | ISBN 9781250183200 (ebook)
Subjects: LCSH: East Indian Americans—Fiction.
Classification: LCC PS3616.A86648 A6 2018 | DDC 813/.6—dc23
LC record available at https://lccn.loc.gov/2018001437

Our books may be purchased in bulk for promotional, educational, or business use. Please contact your local bookseller or the Macmillan Corporate and Premium Sales Department at 1-800-221-7945, extension 5442, or by email at MacmillanSpecialMarkets@macmillan.com.

First Edition: July 2018

10 9 8 7 6 5 4 3 2 1

For my parents

Remember that you and I made this journey, that we went together to a place where there was nowhere left to go.

—Jhumpa Lahiri, *The Namesake*

Contents

If You See Me, Don't Say Hi

god of destruction

The Wi-Fi was out: that was the first sign. The second was that my dress was an eyesore. Online it had appeared chic and trendy, but in person, at the mall, it was an egregious mistake.

"Bachelorette party?" the saleslady had asked.

"First date," I'd said.

His name was Vibash, and we'd met online, through a dating website for Indians called Shaadi.com. He was an engineer. He was thirty-five. He was handsome, with dark hair and dusky skin. The first time he messaged me, I told him all about my job as an interior designer, making it sound glamorous and important, even though it wasn't. It was depressing. Sometimes I would come home after staring at a blank wall for hours, wondering what to mount on it, and imagine my clients' lives unfolding without me. Once, during a renovation, I took the spare key of a doctor's beach house and drove there in the middle of the night. I walked around the large empty space, which was sheeted with plastic, speckled with tape, and imagined myself living in it—with a husband, a dog, a child who looked vaguely like me. I stole a bottle of wine from their refrigerator and drank it in the front seat of my car. Then I backed into their mailbox.

I wasn't always this way. But the friction of life has a way of turning sharp edges into smooth ones, smooth edges into sharp ones, until you've become a duller, slightly misshapen version of your former self. I used to be happy, in the way that people on Facebook seem happy, posting pictures of their husbands and friends. I was the kind of woman who would say things like "I hope you get that promotion" or "I'm sorry about your grandmother" and actually mean it. No one ever told me that happiness was like a currency: that when it goes, it goes, and that few people are willing to give you some of theirs.

The cable guy showed up at seven forty-five. It was dark outside, black clouds hovering low to the ground. He looked Latin, or Persian, with a thick, scruffy beard. I stared at the tattoo on his arm—a skeleton of a mermaid surrounded by a school of dead fish—then up at his face.

"The Wi-Fi is out," I said, closing the door behind us.

He followed me into the living room, where my modem sat next to a pile of indiscriminate wires. He looked me up and down. "Are you going to a party?"

"Excuse me?"

"The dress," he said, smiling. "It looks like you're about to hit the town."

I went upstairs and examined myself in the mirror. Earlier that evening, Vibash had asked me to send him more pictures, so I did: me on a sailboat, me on the beach, me looking sad, then happy, then cross, all in a little frame I'd put up on Instagram. He didn't respond, and I thought I would die. Then, just as I was about to delete him from my cell phone, my email, my life, he said I was beautiful. And it was funny how it could happen: how just like that you could live again.

I went back down and found the cable guy standing in a pile of thick cords and wires and plastic tubing. His tool belt was on the floor. His name was stitched across his chest in bright blue lettering: RICKY A. I wondered what the A was short for. Alvarez? Alvarado? I was famished.

"Are you almost done?"

"What? Oh, yeah. I just gotta clip this wire here and . . ."

I went back into the kitchen and poured myself a glass of wine. I thought about Vibash, about his thick dark hair that was graying at the sides, his wire-framed glasses, his black Mercedes-Benz. He was six foot two—tall for an Indian—with a fine build and ropey muscles. His profile included a picture of him running a marathon, and the way the sweat had poured down his front, darkening his shorts, had made my thighs turn to water.

I was thinking about this when I felt Ricky A.'s presence behind me. He was standing in the half-light, staring at a picture of Lord Shiva on the windowsill. His blue face stared back at us, serenely.

"Are you Hindu?"

"What?"

"This picture. It's a Hindu god, right? Are you?"

"No," I said. "I mean yes, maybe. I guess so. My mother put that there."

"My cousin is a Hindu; he converted. He lives in Orange County with a bunch of guys in an ashram. Are you close?"

"Excuse me?"

"You and your mom. Are you two close?"

It was a personal question to ask, practically vulgar, and yet I found myself answering. "I don't know. We used to be, back when I was engaged. Then my fiancé canceled the wedding and now she looks at me like I'm an alien."

I wondered if he, too, would look at me differently. We stood like that for a while, Ricky and I, gazing at the picture of Lord Shiva, trying to decipher what lay behind his enigmatic smile, when my cell phone broke the silence. It was Vibash; he was waiting.

"Look, is it fixed or not?" I asked.

"Oh, sure. Why don't you check it out for yourself?"

Ricky A. followed me into the living room. I opened my laptop. I could feel his eyes on the back of my head. I could smell his cologne, too—a cheap-smelling fragrance that reminded me of the boys I went to high school with. I was nervous. I covered up my screen with my hand, embarrassed by the Match.com profile that suddenly popped up in the window. "Yep—it works."

"Are you sure?"

"Yes, I'm sure," I said. "Look, I really have to go now."

He followed me to the door. He scribbled something onto a receipt. Then he handed it over. "This is my cell," he said. "If it acts up again, you just call me." He stared at me for a moment, as if he were about to say something more; then he stepped out into the night. "Have fun at your party."

Two years ago, I had it all: a successful career, a doting fiancé, and an army of well-wishers. I didn't realize the former two determined the latter. After Amal broke up with me, my friends dropped off like flies, making excuses for their absences: emergencies and scheduling conflicts and some horrific but convenient catastrophes. Thank god for Valerie. We went from drunken sorority girls to drunken adults, functioning through our alcoholism. Then one day she got a boyfriend—Doug—and everything changed. Once, we were having brunch together when I asked Valerie if she ever wondered if Doug was gay.

"Excuse me?"

"You know." I smiled. "The mannerisms."

"What mannerisms?"

She dropped her croissant on the table.

"Well, the way he moves, for one, and the way he talks, and his voice. It's kind of nasally, right?"

I laughed, doing an impersonation. She stared at me.

"I don't know what you mean."

I was only joking about him being gay; I only sort-of thought he was gay. I wouldn't have said anything at all if Valerie hadn't been going on about the engagement ring they'd seen at Tiffany, and how it was perfect, and how Doug had wanted a destination wedding because that way fewer people would attend. I just wanted to inject a little humor back into our lives, the way we did when we were girls, when life and all its disappointments were a million miles away from us.

She said it was best if we didn't speak to each other for a while.

My Uber driver—Siddharth was his name—was lost.

"I am following directions and round and round we are going."

It was dark out, stars glimmering across the sky like handfuls of spilled salt. I was an hour late.

"Listen," I said. "How long is this going to take? We were supposed to be there ten minutes ago."

He glanced at his wristwatch.

"Jesus Christ," I said. "I might as well have driven myself."

For weeks, while Vibash and I messaged each other, I had dreamt of this moment: at the office, the gym, while listening to music in the shower. My previous experiences with dating had been disappointments—awkward dinners with stilted conversation—but Vibash was showing signs of promise. We already shared all the things in common two people could possibly share: a love of foreign films, hip-hop music, and Japanese food. We'd already had the requisite conversations, in which we divulged every embarrassing story from our youth. We'd already told each other about the romantic failures we'd had, the mistakes we'd made, and, at thirty-four, I had already begun to imagine myself as a bride again, wearing the gold and ruby jewelry my mother had brought back from India, shortly before Amal and I split up.

It was pathetic.

It was also premature. I made it to the bar and scanned the crowd of well-dressed men and women drinking chardonnay in their various shades of black, but Vibash wasn't there. He wasn't in the bathroom, either, and, after waiting for twenty minutes, my foolish hope began to deflate, like a voluminous hairstyle that fell flat on my head. Then a strange man looked at me from across the bar, smiling. "Are you looking for someone?"

"Yes," I said. "I am."

He pulled out a napkin.

"Are you Anita Gun . . ."

"Gundapaneni," I said. "Yes, that's me."

He handed me the napkin. "He left this for you."

I stared at it until the words blurred and split in two, then snapped back into focus.

Sorry. Didn't see you. Had to leave.

My heart sank. I sent him a text message, Hey, come back! and waited for him by the bar.

He never showed up.

He didn't respond to my text, either, and, after waiting for thirty minutes, I decided to give up, ordering another Uber home. I was relieved when the driver turned out to be a young white woman with colored streaks in her hair. She drove a Mazda, and she was listening to a song from my past: "Where Do You Go" by No Mercy. Valerie and I used to dance to it in her room:

Where do you go, my lovely?
I wanna know.

I thought about calling Valerie and playing the song for her over the phone, but then I pictured her at home, with Doug, watching Netflix, some contrived film she would later rave about over yoga, or brunch, or at a dinner party I wasn't invited to, and I fell asleep.

"Miss, we're here."

We were sitting outside my house. It was pitch-black. I let myself in, dropping my keys on the console and slipping off my heels. I poured myself a glass of wine. I didn't need it, but I was thirsty. All night I had been poised for it to happen, the transition, the moment my life would change forever. And now it hadn't. And everything was the same. I walked over to my laptop and went on Match.com, scrolling through my messages. Then I remembered that it was Amal's birthday. I'd seen it on Facebook earlier. I thought about calling him. It was a habit of ours, when we were dating, to be the first ones to greet each other on our birthdays whenever we were apart. I saw my cell phone sitting on the countertop next to my handbag and, when I made my way toward it, I tripped over something on the floor. I stared at it. It was a tool belt. I knelt down and examined it in my hands. It was made of dark leather and it smelled faintly of Old Spice, but I couldn't remember where it had come from, or how it had ended up on my living room floor.

And then, just like that, I did.

I went into the kitchen and grabbed my bag, searching for his number. I emptied the contents: Chapstick, eye cream, a firming lotion from Macy's, two lipsticks in the shades of coral and mauve. I couldn't find it. I was overcome with a kind of desperation. If I find the number, I thought, I will be saved. If I find the number, Vibash will text me back. If I find the number, my life up until now won't have been a mistake.

I found it: it was stuck to a gum wrapper with a piece of chewed-up gum in it. I dialed it at once. I stood in the living room, waiting and waiting and waiting, until he answered on the fourth ring.

"Hello?"

"Ricky?"

"Huh?"

He sounded tired. I glanced at my wristwatch and realized it was 12:30 A.M.

"You came to my house earlier, to fix my Wi-Fi?"

I heard some commotion in the background: the sound of a

drawer banging shut, the bark of a dog, the chink of glass against wood, and finally, his deep, guttural sigh.

"Yeah?"

"You left something behind."

He was silent.

"A tool belt," I said. "You can pick it up if you want. I'm home now."

"Right now?"

"Sure."

He seemed to consider this. "Shit, it's after midnight."

"I have insomnia," I said. "I've had it for years. I don't even need sleep, really." I was overcome with a sense of urgency. It had to be now, I thought to myself. It had to happen now. "Plus," I continued, almost breathlessly, "my Wi-Fi is out again."

He must have heard the desperation in my voice—he must have known—because within moments he was telling me to stay right there, that he would be right over. I unplugged some wires and spilled some wine on them just to be sure. Then I retouched my hair.

He arrived twenty minutes later, wearing the same shirt as before, as if he'd only grabbed it off the floor and sniffed it to make sure it was clean. I glanced at his tattoo, then up at his face.

"I'm glad you could come."

He walked into the living room and picked up the tool belt and knelt down in front of the modem. I didn't want to be near him when he discovered the unplugged wires, so I told him I would be upstairs.

"Just holler when you're done."

Only I fell asleep. I'd meant to simply rest my head, which was throbbing as if I'd banged it against a kitchen cabinet. I was still in my dress, my hair a bird's nest of curls, when Ricky A. walked into the room.

"Sorry, ma'am. You didn't answer. I'm all done down there. The cords were damaged. I replaced them with new ones—it's all set to go now."

He hesitated a moment before retreating. "So I guess I'll be leaving then."

I was too tired to speak, to tell him to stay, but then I heard his footsteps on the staircase and was jolted awake.

"Wait," I said, running down the stairs.

He was lacing up his boots when I stumbled into the hall. "Would you like a drink?"

It was clear what I was offering, the full, unbridled scope of it, and yet he crinkled his brows.

"Right now?"

"Sure," I said. "As a thank-you. It's the least I can do."

He mulled this over for a while, as if he wasn't quite sure what to make of it. Then he slipped his boots off and placed them neatly by the door.

"A drink," he said, thinking. "Yeah, sure. A drink sounds good."

As it turned out, we had more to discuss than I thought. Ricky A. was funny, in the way that younger, attractive men can sometimes be funny. We sat across from each other in the breakfast nook and he told me stories about all the crazy shit he had seen as a cable guy, things you could never imagine, that would only happen on TV. I wondered if he thought that this, too, seemed crazy. He drank a beer, and there was a bit of foam hanging on to the slick dark tinsel of his beard. I was tempted to reach out and wipe it, but this was the type of bold gesture I was incapable of making, so I let it hang there for a while, nodding and laughing at all the appropriate intervals. I talked about myself: my checkered past, my road to becoming a designer, Amal and all the various ways in which we had disappointed one another. I wondered if he thought I was pathetic, if he would tell his friends later about the sad old woman he'd slept with, who wouldn't shut the fuck up. Then I realized that in actuality I was a lot bolder than I thought I was, that everything I'd done in my life was a form of mild rebellion, and that, in the grand scheme of things, the opinions of people like Ricky A. didn't matter, not in the end. So I did it. I reached over and swiped my finger across his lips, allowing it to linger against the wet pink surface of his tongue.

"You had foam on your mouth," I said.

He licked his lips and leaned in close so there would be no mistaking it, so that I could see the intensity in his eyes when he told me this:

"I know—I was waiting for you to do that."

We went to my bedroom and started kissing. I switched off the lights. Ricky A. switched them back on.

"No. I want to see you."

There was a sudden gravity in his tone, as if, in the time it took to wander upstairs, he had grown a bit, become more of a man, as if all the innocence from before was just an act, a performance.

I was melting inside.

"I haven't been to the gym," I said, shyly. And then, "How old are you?"

Ricky A. laughed. He took off his shirt. His body was brown and muscled, with tattoos everywhere, on his chest and his stomach and his back. A line of thick dark hair traveled down his belly and disappeared into the waistband of his shorts.

"How old do I look?"

"Nineteen?"

He laughed again. "Take your dress off."

I did as I was told, wiggling out of it in a sort-of dance, aware of how the roles had quickly reversed, how it was *he* who was suddenly in control. He stared at me baldly, taking me in.

"Now your bra."

I couldn't remember the last time I had been naked in front of a man, and yet there was power in this, exposing myself to someone I had no interest in, who would never know the inner workings of my life. I flung my bra over the bed and, without him asking, my panties, too. He brought them close to his face.

"You smell amazing."

"I do?"

"Like flowers."

"Really?"

"Oh, yeah."

I smiled, vindicated. Then I asked him again, "How old are you?"

He said he was twenty-two.

He spent the night. I wanted him to. He pressed his naked body against mine and we stayed like that for hours. I had a dream that Ricky A. was actually a Ph.D. student who worked as a cable guy on weekends just to pay the bills, that we were married in a small but tasteful ceremony, and that we had three beautiful little girls. I woke up with a smile on my lips, turning over to nuzzle my face against the dark damp nest of his armpit, when I realized he was gone.

"Ricky?"

I sat up in bed, scanning the walls for his patchwork body, but he wasn't in the room. I rubbed my eyes and discovered that his clothes were still in a pile on the floor. His wallet was still on the nightstand. His thick white socks were still hanging from the floor lamp. I could still smell him on my sheets, a mix of cologne and sweat that would remain until I did the washing, which wasn't very often. I walked downstairs. Ricky was staring at the picture of Lord Shiva on the windowsill, picking it up in his hands, when he noticed me and smiled.

"Good morning."

He opened his arms to hug me and I knew, by the way my body went limp in his embrace, that I wanted him gone.

"Thanks, Ricky," I said. "For everything."

It was at this particular moment that his expression suddenly changed.

"Oh yeah," he said, wincing. "About that. My name—it's not Ricky."

"What?"

"You kept saying it last night, and I didn't want to disappoint you, in case it was some sort of fantasy. But that's not my real name. Not even close. My real name is Ernesto."

"But your shirt," I said.

He shook his head. "That's just a generic name. The company doesn't want us to use our real ones. They definitely don't want some guy going around introducing himself as Ernesto." He laughed heartily.

I lowered my gaze. "Oh."

I was strangely disappointed, as if this sudden revelation negated everything that had happened to me the night before, as if the real Ricky A. was still out there, waiting for me. I also knew that I would never see him again. I occupied myself in the kitchen while Ernesto went upstairs and put on his clothes and washed his face and brushed his teeth with his finger, singing and splashing all the while. Then I followed him to the door. Outside, the morning light was bright, the sun blasting through the clouds like brilliant shards of glass.

"Can I call you?" Ernesto said. "Can we hang out?"

"Sure," I replied—though I knew that we wouldn't, that it was a mistake I would never make again—and I watched him jump into his Chevy Tahoe and disappear down the road.

I have never told Vibash any of this. I was too embarrassed. He called two days later, to ask for a second chance, and we agreed to meet at a restaurant overlooking the water, and a coffee shop the next day, and a movie theater the following weekend. We kept meeting, at restaurants and bars, theaters and nightclubs, playgrounds and parlors, until six months later, when he asked me to move in. It became a legend: the story of our failed first date. Sometimes I would start to tell it, and Vibash would chime in, filling in the gaps. I would cringe when he got to the part about leaving the bar—he had no idea what I had done. No one did. I kept it to myself, wincing whenever a colleague happened to say something positively bland like "What a night!" or "I guess it was meant to be!" I would nod along and smile, resting my head against Vibash's shoulder. It was something I did quite often: the nodding and smiling. After canceling my lease, I packed my things in boxes and moved into Vibash's slate-colored house. It had a smooth green lawn and a patio with a pool, and sometimes I liked to lie there with a glass of white wine. I redecorated his house with beaded wallpaper and off-white lacquer. Vibash installed a security system. We threw a party for our friends—the dentists and doctors and lawyers, the engineers at Vibash's firm—and later, after everyone had left, he surprised me with a ring. I had mended fences with Valerie and some of the other women I had offended during the course of my misery, and was subsequently flattered when they ushered me back into their lives. With their help, I became a new woman, adorned with certainty, varnished with pride, glittering with the trappings of a shared life. Sometimes I looked at old pictures of myself and wondered where all the misery went, if it was still lurking somewhere deep inside. Now, whenever I posted a picture of myself on Facebook, Vibash was there, standing by my side, his arm wrapped lovingly around my shoulder, his hand clasped tightly in mine. At night, I stared at these pictures for hours, reading the comments that proliferated like weeds beneath them, bolstered whenever someone happened to post something positive, offended when they didn't.

I was doing this one evening when the Wi-Fi went out again.

It was late, and Vibash and I were watching a documentary on Netflix. The screen halted, and Vibash walked over to the modem and picked it up in his hands.

"The Wi-Fi is out," he said. He unplugged the modem and waited a few moments before plugging it back in again. But it didn't work. "Goddamn it. We were just getting started. I'll have to call the cable company now."

He flipped through a phone book and walked into the kitchen. I heard his voice in the hall. He returned with a smile.

"They said they can send someone over in fifteen minutes. That's pretty fast."

I finished my glass of wine, quickly pouring another one. Vibash was staring at me.

"Easy there."

I glanced at my wristwatch and the sunset outside, which smoldered behind a row of black, lacy trees. The doorbell rang. Vibash ran to answer it. I sat down on the couch, examining a mysterious stain on the carpet—red wine, or maybe one of Vibash's protein shakes—when he walked into the room.

He looked the same, except he was wearing a different-colored shirt, and his name wasn't Ricky anymore; it was Ted. Vibash chatted with him in the foyer before leading him into the house. He didn't look at me. He went straight to the modem. Vibash was still talking about the documentary he and I were watching, something about Vikings or samurais or spies, when he looked at me and smiled.

I dropped my glass of wine.

"Jesus, Anita," Vibash said. "What's wrong?"

The glass shattered against the smooth slate floor, and red wine pooled at my feet. Vibash went into the kitchen to fetch towels and napkins and a portable vacuum cleaner, leaving the two of us alone.

"So," Ernesto said, "how long have you and your husband been in this house?" He was staring at the blank walls beyond us, the vaulted ceiling above, and I realized, suddenly, that he had no idea who I was.

"Just a couple months," I said. "And he's not my husband."

"Oh."

"He's my fiancé," I said, "and we're getting married next year."

"Congratulations."

He stared at me without the slightest trace of recognition.

Then he turned and examined the bookcase next to the modem that housed our statues and albums and books. He picked something up in his hands, and I knew, even before he had the chance to look at me with a curious arch of his brow, what it was: the picture of Lord Shiva. I had always hated it, but Vibash insisted we display it in public, in case my mother ever came to visit. "This is beautiful," he said. Vibash returned with the towels. The Wi-Fi was up and running again. Ernesto picked up the remote control and reloaded the documentary. It seemed to me, in that moment at least, that we stood like that for a very long time, all three of us, waiting for it to start. ♦

hare rama, hare krishna

On Fridays my mother made chicken curry for my father and me. Later, she cooked only for me. The curry was still there; my father was not. He'd moved, not to Cleveland or Indianapolis, but to a one-story house on Devonshire Drive. Often, and with no relevant provocation, my mother brought up his other woman, referring to her as "that lady." That lady performed black magic. That lady ruined our lives. That lady won't get a dime of his money—just you wait and see. That lady was ten years younger than my mother. At twenty-seven, she wasn't much of a "lady" at all.

Her name was Lisa. She was my father's secretary. I remember the first time I met her, when I was eleven years old. She was lank, and blond, with glass-colored eyes. Her skin was translucent. She wore chic clothes, far more expensive than anything my mother owned—this in spite of the fact that my father was an ophthalmologist, that we lived in one of the largest homes in our town. My mother was simple—her copper skin without makeup, her dark hair in a braid. When she saw Lisa standing in our foyer that bright summer afternoon, painted and coiffed like a doll, she turned up her nose. "I don't trust her," she said, not to my father, but to me. I laughed at her—my mother didn't trust anyone—but she was right: six months later, Lisa called our house in the middle of the night.

"What is it?" my mother asked, after my father had hung up the phone.

"It's Lisa," he said. "She's complaining about a sharp pain in her eye."

I heard my parents argue: Why couldn't she go to the emergency room? Why did she have to call the house? Why did my father speak to her in such an intimate way? Why, at the very least, didn't she go to the hospital instead? I heard the hum of my father's Jaguar and saw the flicker of its taillights down the road.

Then I heard the slam of a door.

My parents didn't speak much after that. My father left for work early each morning, returning late in the night. Sometimes he didn't come home at all. Once, he called to say that he had gone to San Francisco for a medical conference; he would be home in a few days. My mother was furious. She spent long afternoons complaining about my father to her sisters over the phone. She prayed three times a day. Sometimes she buried strange objects in our backyard: a coconut decorated with vermilion, a handful of rice, marigold petals that spilled from her hands.

In the end, my father didn't deny it. My mother found the love letters Lisa had written to him in the glove compartment of his car. She wanted a divorce. I was surprised. I had heard my mother criticizing other women in our town—women who drank cocktails and divorced their husbands at the drop of a hat. My mother was not that kind of woman. She was faithful. They'd had an arranged marriage; it would never have occurred to her to leave. She was religious, too, leaving trails of incense all over the house.

Sometimes she left strange items in the pockets of my jeans: a picture of Lord Krishna, a fragment of ash, a piece of fruit from the temple *prasad*.

"Don't go stepping on your books," she would say, if I happened to be arranging them on the living room floor. "Everything you learned will be gone."

They agreed to separate. My father moved into Lisa's apartment; my mother looked for a job. She cursed them from my room.

"Good-for-nothings," she said.

I ignored her. With my father gone, I saw no reason to please her. In fact, I blamed her. If only she had been the type of woman Lisa was—if only she didn't wear those god-awful clothes. I tried to help her, once, suggesting she buy a short black dress from the mall, but she refused. "What sort of boy has an interest in clothes?"

I did—shoes, too, and Bollywood films. My favorite actress was Madhuri Dixit. I danced to her songs in my room. I stood in front of my mirror with my belly exposed, my T-shirt over my head, the ends of which flowed down my back like a wig. Every now and then, I borrowed one of my mother's saris and pretended to dance in the rain. Once, I imagined a pair of hands traveling over my naked body, massaging my breasts, at which point I got an erection, putting everything away.

Unbeknownst to my mother, I spent long hours admiring Lisa from afar: the glint of her hair, the gloss of her legs, the effortless way she dressed, as if she'd only happened to find a gold and turquoise bracelet that matched perfectly with her blouse. Sometimes, at the office, Lisa entertained me while I waited for my father to finish a consultation. She knew about the things that consumed my life: X-Men and Game Boy and Bell Biv DeVoe.

We sang along to "Poison" in the back of the office, after all the patients had left, the door to the reception area closed, the blinds shut tight. My father joined in afterward, and the glassy look in his eyes, the way he laughed with his entire body, expressed a love for her I had never witnessed before.

It didn't last. Eventually, Lisa and my father split up. I don't know why. Maybe Lisa grew bored with him. Maybe she grew weary of being his mistress. He never brought her around to the Indian functions in our town: dinner parties in the basement of some doctor's home. He never spoke of her in public. He never allowed her to get out of the car when he picked me up from my house. The last I'd heard, she was attending art school in Chicago. My father returned, penitent, requesting to move back in. But my mother refused. She had no use for him now.

So they remained married but separated. My father moved into the house down the street from us. He drove me to school. Sometimes he came over to mow the lawn or pay the bills. Once a week, he joined us at the dinner table for a curry or a dal, but he never spent the night. Both he and my mother showed up to my parent-teacher conferences and asked after my grades. To the outside world, to the cousins and teachers and uncles and aunts, they were still a couple, still husband and wife, still bound together by me, their only child. Had anyone understood the true nature of their arrangement, the reason for their separation, they would've been appalled. I suspect this pleased my mother. It gave her power. As long as my father was alone, as long as he turned up to our dinners every Saturday night, she would always be in control.

In the fall of senior year, I had to choose a physical activity, so I chose dance. It was the only way I could get out of gym. I registered for an evening class that met twice a week in a dance studio at the center of town. It was October when I took my first class. The air smelled like burnt leaves. I liked this time of year: when you had to sleep with an extra blanket on your bed. I liked that the sky got all dark and smeary, and the leaves turned to fireballs. I liked that every month had a holiday. I was applying to colleges that year. It was nice to know that, at the end of the month, I could dress up as Spider-Man.

The class was called Urban Groove. The flyer showed a young man wearing track pants and a hooded sweatshirt, spinning on his head. I had tried spinning once—breaking, too. I learned all the moves. I re-created them at school dances and everyone called me "MJ Kapoor." This was before the incident with Jordan Mann in the boys' locker room, after which they just called me a queer.

The whole thing was a mistake. We were changing in the locker room when I happened to notice the smattering of dark brown hair that stemmed from Jordan's navel. I turned my head. I stared at it again. I couldn't stop staring. He was swiping a stick of deodorant under his arms, talking to one of his friends, when all of a sudden someone shoved me from behind.

"Faggot."

It was Brendan Simmons. His hair was the color of orange shag carpeting; his skin was the color of boiled shrimp. He narrowed his eyes.

"I always knew you were a queer."

"Samir the queer," someone said.

"Samir the queer," Brendan echoed, shoving me again. "I like that."

For weeks thereafter, Brendan tormented me in the halls, shouting "Samir the queer" whenever I walked past. He waited for me in the locker room before issuing a warning to everyone around: "Put your dicks away, fellas. It's Samir the queer." Sometimes he pushed me from behind, or flicked me on my ear, or tripped me in the halls, or rallied his friends so they could throw me into the shower. Once, he went up to Jordan Mann and gave him a ring. "It's from Samir, man. He wanted me to give it to you." He said nothing for a while, just stared at the ring, stared at Brendan, stared at me. Then he walked out of the room.

For weeks I was besotted. I saw Jordan in the halls, walking alone to class, a backpack slung over his left shoulder, white sneakers on his feet. He dressed in tight-fitting sweaters over indigo jeans. His chestnut hair was always swept to the side. He never said more than a word or two all day. Once, before an exam, I asked to borrow a pencil. It was our English midterm, and Jordan was sitting at the desk in front of me. The fabric of his T-shirt clung like film to his muscles as he reached into his backpack and tossed the pencil onto my desk. That night, when I found the pencil stuck in my back pocket, I dialed his number. I'd looked it up in the phone book, memorizing it by heart. My mother was out running errands. The phone rang and rang, and, just as I was about to hang up, Jordan's voice came on at the other end.

"Jordan?" I said.

"Yeah."

"I have your pencil."

"Huh?"

"Your pencil?" The blood rushed to my face. "I borrowed it for the exam. I wanted to tell you that I have it. I didn't steal it or anything. I'll give it back to you tomorrow."

There was silence, during which I contemplated the very purpose of my life. Then Jordan started laughing.

"Oh, shit," he said. "Samir, man. You can keep it. No worries."

I was embarrassed but buoyed. I hung up the phone and

placed the pencil next to a stack of comic books on my desk. All night long, I imagined us becoming friends, exchanging notes during class, playing Street Fighter at the video arcade. I saw us wearing matching outfits during "twin day" at our school. I was dizzy with the possibilities, unable to sleep, skipping breakfast the next morning so that I'd be early to school. But when I walked into English class, Jordan barely acknowledged me, and when I sat down behind him, he inched forward in his seat. It was as if our conversation the night before had never even happened, as if I had made the entire thing up in my head.

At home, my parents regarded me with blissful ignorance, unaware of my life at school. Beyond my grades—and the requirement that I attend college in the fall—they expressed little concern for my social affairs. Once, at the mall, Brendan Simmons shouted an insult from across the store. "Your friend is calling you," my mother said, holding a blouse to her neck. "Go play." If a child my age laughed at me, my mother would nudge me from behind. "Go play." When the neighborhood kids threw rocks at my head, my mother would ask if I had enjoyed their game. Only during moments of extreme frustration—when I lingered too long over the stove, when I listened to her conversations over the phone, when I stared at her pinning the filigreed pleats of her sari to her blouse—would she turn her sharp focus onto me. "What sort of boy does these things?"

I had no answer. My father didn't, either. He occupied his time at the house doing chores, fixing the plumbing in the bathroom or a leak on the roof. His only form of communication was at the dinner table on Saturday evenings when he would raise his palm to indicate that he was full, refusing the extra helping of chicken or lamb my mother was offering. At the end of the meal, he took a handful of *mawa*—fenugreek seeds mixed with candies and mints—and chewed them silently while watching the news. At ten o'clock he would leave, taking with him the sharp scent of his cologne, the slight heft of his weight, the dark veil of guilt he now wore like a hood, like a shroud.

My first class was at 5 P.M. on a Friday. I was the only boy. I was pretty sure I was going to quit. The choreography was less intricate than I had imagined. The routine was nothing more than a series of steps, really, embellished here and there with a ball change. I had expected something different. I had hoped to learn the choreography from Michael Jackson's "Remember the Time." I had imagined doing windmills on the floor. I had not imagined this.

The instructor's name was Anton. He was Filipino. He wove a path around us and enumerated our steps. The other kids were flustered, bumping into each other, but not me. I added my own take: a body roll, a hip thrust, a two-step where there was one. Anton frowned.

"No need for flair," he said. "Just keep it simple—keep it clean."

There was a mirror at the front of the room in which I could observe the other students, so I folded my arms, watching them. Then a door swung open; a figure emerged. I turned my head. It was Jordan. He walked into the room wearing shorts and a tight white T-shirt, his hair slicked back, dripping at the ends. I was stunned.

He noticed me watching him and nodded his head. I hadn't anticipated his world to crash so effortlessly into mine. I wasn't prepared for Jordan to sit down next to me and cross his legs, smiling at me. He smelled like rain—I heard the gentle drumming of it on the rooftop above our heads—and something sweeter, like bodywash or shampoo.

"It's coming down out there," he said.

I glanced at the bare wall as if it were a window through which I could see outside to the shimmering rain. I nodded. Jordan stretched his arms, his T-shirt lifting slightly to reveal the pale, stubbly surface of his belly. I turned my head.

I thought about him all weekend: at the dinner table, at the mall, while my mother cooked curry on the stove. I thought about him while watching Bollywood movies in my room. I thought about him, still, that early Sunday morning, when I walked into the kitchen to find my father standing over the stove.

"Where's Mom?" I said.

"In the bath."

"When did you get here?"

He didn't answer me.

"I'm frying bacon," he said.

The bacon hissed and sputtered in its pan. The kitchen filled with smoke. I watched him curiously. He had aged since the separation, since Lisa had run away. His eye bags were puffed; his once black hair was now speckled with gray. I took my seat at the breakfast table and folded my arms. He piled the bacon onto my plate.

The following Monday, Jordan walked into class just as Anton was teaching us the second eight count to "Dangerous" by Busta Rhymes. He removed his coat and took a place across the room. I was disappointed. I wanted him to join *me*—I had spread myself out for this exclusive purpose, causing one of the girls to trip over her feet. She was looking at Jordan now; we all were. He wore light gray shorts that grew dark with sweat as the lesson progressed, his muscles bulging, his hair turning slick. I watched him closely. He was good, though not as good as me. There was something tentative about the way he moved, as if he were counting each step, anticipating the transitions before they even happened. Soon, the class was over and everyone filed out of the room. Jordan hung back, waiting for me.

"You were great," he said, his face damp with sweat. "I'm serious. You should be teaching the class instead."

My heart jumped. We walked outside and started talking about things I no longer remember, things I would attempt to recall later, wishing I could. It was dark out, and our faces were lit by the overhead lights. Jordan lit a cigarette.

"I'm only taking this to get out of gym," he said.

"Me, too."

He nodded. Blue smoke curled from his lips. Jordan told me he had to walk five blocks to catch the bus—his car was in the shop. So I offered him a ride.

The drive was quiet, Jordan pointing at darkened signs, telling me which way to turn. I sensed his presence the way one senses a strange noise in the house. I couldn't believe he was sitting next to me. I asked him about college.

"I'm taking a year off to travel."

I was surprised. I had imagined Jordan would enroll in an Ivy League school, Princeton or Brown, where he would study finance or chemistry or physics or law—I did this often, projecting the futures of my classmates onto the blank canvas of my own.

"We have our whole lives to finish college," Jordan said. "I'm only eighteen."

I turned in to his neighborhood, imagining us taking snapshots in front of the Eiffel Tower, Jordan in a white tank top, me in a fancy suit. I made a left onto his street. The houses looked familiar: brick and wood structures with bay windows and French doors.

"It's the house at the end," he said. "With the brick mailbox."

I pulled in to his drive, switching off the car. Jordan thanked me for the ride. Then he reached over the gearshift and kissed me on the mouth.

When I got home my parents were drinking red wine on the sofa. I could tell by my father's smile that he was drunk. I went upstairs for my bath. I sank into soapy water, remembering the way Jordan's lips had felt against my own. I couldn't believe it. But I had to. I had to remember every last detail: the texture of his lips, the taste of his mouth, the song that came on the radio after I pulled out of Jordan's drive. I rinsed myself in warm, fragrant water, playing it over in my head.

That night, I heard my parents whispering about something in the kitchen, raising their voices in the hall, and later, in the bedroom, their soft moans, penetrating the wall.

They said nothing about it the next morning. My father was in his business suit. My mother was in her robe. The makeup she had worn the night before was smudged around the eyes. She wore more makeup now: lipsticks and shadows and brightening creams. I found shopping bags all over the house filled with bright, velvety things. My father started coming around more often, taking us to dinner, watching movies with us in the den, inviting my mother out with him on Sunday afternoons, to go shopping at the mall. Their rekindled companionship left me with free time on my hands—time I spent at Jordan's house, kissing on his bed. His parents were rarely home. When they were, we snuck into the basement and Jordan locked the door. I had locked my own door, once, to look at a dirty magazine. My mother had screamed at me to open it.

I was surprised, then, by her sudden indifference. She never asked me where I was. She was too busy planning the meals she would prepare or the movies she would rent or the sweaters and blouses she would wear in my father's presence. She colored her hair. "I never said it was over," she said, to her sisters over the phone. "He's my husband, after all."

At school, Jordan and I kept our friendship private, especially from Brendan Simmons—who continued to tease me, shouting insults at the back of my head. But I no longer listened. Every now and then, Jordan walked by me in the halls and I felt his fingertips grazing my skin. He left notes in my locker. He called every evening. At football games we sought each other out across the thickening crowd. And of course there was dance. Had anyone noticed? I wondered if they did, if they paid attention to the way we looked at each other, laughing at the same moments, over precisely the same things. I wondered what they would say if they found out, if our bodies had betrayed us in a way our mouths never would.

Then one day, I was making a peanut butter and jelly sandwich in the kitchen when my mother came down the stairs.

"That boy called."

Her hair was damp from the bath, the silk panel of her dressing gown dark in certain spots. It was a cold morning in January, and she shivered as she lit a wick of incense and set it onto the counter.

"Which boy?"

"That boy. The one that keeps calling."

I stared at her. I cut the crusts off my sandwich and sliced it into halves, then fourths. "Jordan," I said.

"Jordan," she echoed. "Where does he live?"

"In the neighborhood."

"How did you meet?"

"At school."

"What do his parents do?"

"They're professors."

She paused, nodding. "I see."

I could tell by her tone that the information was satisfactory; having established Jordan's background, he was now a suitable friend. I considered telling her the truth: that, just the other day, Jordan had slipped his finger over my tongue and asked for a blow job. I told her I was late for dance instead.

I skipped dance, though, and went straight to Jordan's house. He offered me a beer. We drank it on the sofa while listening to Lauryn Hill. He looked at me with a determined glaze in his eyes, as if he were about to reveal some grave and irrevocable truth.

"I'm going to Brazil," he said. "I booked my ticket last night. I'll be leaving in the fall."

My heart sank. I imagined Jordan on the beach, his hair woven into knots, and a sense of longing lodged deep in my bones. I was not going to Brazil. I was going to Brown, where I had been accepted two weeks earlier, and where I would major in chemistry—not dance—according to my parents.

Jordan laughed. "Life's too short for chemistry."

He kissed me on my lips, and the smell of him—like soap and skin—seeped into my clothes. I would catch flashes of that smell long after he was gone, at the supermarket, at the mall, in my bedroom even, holding the pillow close to my chest. We were silent for a while, Jordan's head pressed against my own, then he whispered something in my ear. "Do you think about me?" He paused, uncertain. "When I'm not around?"

I told him I did.

I had expected my mother to be up and angry—my curfew was at ten—but when I walked into the living room she was nowhere to be found. The next morning, she was humming to herself in the kitchen as if nothing was wrong. "I'll need you to go to the store," she said. "I'm cooking dinner for your father."

She tore off a grocery list and pressed it into my palm.

After school, I went to the grocery store and picked up chilies and ginger and garlic and cloves, the organic chicken my father would lick clean from the bone. I stopped by the deli, where a woman was assessing a colorful array of seafood, silver-skinned salmon displayed like jeweled bags.

"Samir?"

She was wearing black silk slacks, a matching black top. A gold necklace sparkled at her throat. It had been six years since I'd seen her, but I recognized her at once.

Of course I did.

"My goodness," she said, approaching me. "Look how you've grown."

It was Lisa. Her blond hair was longer now. Apart from a few wrinkles, she looked exactly the same. She paid for the salmon and walked over to me with open arms, beaming.

"How old are you now?"

"Seventeen."

"Unbelievable."

I wanted to ask her what was so unbelievable about it. I wanted to tell her that *she* was the unbelievable one. I said nothing instead. We stared at the tiled floor. She asked about my parents and I told her they were fine. I didn't tell her the truth: that they were spending every day together, sleeping in the same room, moaning so loudly I'd had to put cotton in my ears.

"I'm starting college soon," I said.

"Really? That's wonderful, Samir. I can't believe how much has changed."

She told me she had taken a job at a local theater in town; she was a dancer. I wondered if she would give me lessons. I was about to ask her this when she hugged me and kissed me and told me to give my parents her regards. Then she was gone, leaving behind the sweet scent of her perfume, the pale sheen of her powder, the faint smudge of her lipstick coloring one side of my face. Later that evening, I unloaded the groceries and watched my mother set three place mats on the table for dinner.

But my father never arrived.

▲▼▲

They'd kept in touch—Lisa had found my father's contact information in a medical journal at her school. I was scandalized. I thought about all the evenings my parents had spent together, the errands on Sunday afternoons. I thought about the moaning, too. I never learned when it happened, at what point Lisa and my father had reunited.

Before long, she was moving her things into my father's house, parking by his curb, attending to the rhododendrons in his front yard. She answered the telephone, with a proprietary lilt my own mother had never possessed. There were no parting words. One evening my father was watching *Lagaan* with us in the den, and the next day he was gone, his shoes missing from the mat, his jackets stripped from the walls, the scent of his cologne fading from the fabric of the sofas and chairs. It was as if everything they'd shared together had been a lie, as if my father had been biding his time, waiting for the precise moment to leave again.

My mother retreated to her room. I wondered if she even bathed. Sometimes she muttered to herself in the kitchen while wiping the same spot of spilled tea. Once, she went through the entire house and removed all the portraits and vacation pictures and piled them onto the living room floor. Then she lit a match, ultimately losing the inspiration, putting everything away. Things began to disappear from the house: the makeup, the wine, the curry on Friday nights, the kebabs my mother marinated and skewered and grilled.

"From now on there will be no meat in this house," she said. "If you want to eat a burger, you can eat it outside!"

I ate them at my father's house instead; Lisa cooked them on the grill. She made sausages, too, and potato salad. They had an intimacy my parents had never possessed, causing me to shy away from them when they held hands in the kitchen, or traded secrets over the stove, or touched each other in that effortless way, or escaped into the bedroom and turned off all the lights. I never spent the night. I imagined Lisa's moans were much louder than my mother's. I also imagined she would be guilty, ashamed of her sudden place in my father's life—in mine—but she wasn't, and neither was my father; in fact, he was smitten, waving their relationship around like a brightly colored flag.

I explained all of this to Jordan in my room, on a Sunday morning, dark clouds gathering outside my window. The house was silent. The jeweled art and plush carpets spoke of excess, but also regret. The windows, wide and full of light, revealed nothing of the darkness that lay within. It was almost noon, and my mother was at the temple. She was praying again. I often woke to the sound of her chanting—Hare Rama, Hare Krishna, Hare Rama, Hare Krishna—until the whole house quaked and shook with her voice. I felt sorry for her, seeking comfort in the cadence of spells. Sometimes I walked by the statue of Lord Krishna in the living room—blue as a robin's egg, with a peacock feather adorning his hair—and felt as if my every movement were being judged. Once, after watching porn, I thought I saw Lord Krishna's shape hovering outside my bedroom window, shaking his head. It was a blue jay.

Jordan fished a joint from his pocket, lighting it in his hands. It was raining, steel rivers blurring the windows above our heads. I lay with my arm on his chest, listening to the sound of the rain sluicing off the sloped roof and onto the slick concrete below.

"I'm taking you with me," he said.

"Where?"

"To Brazil."

I laughed. I thought about Brown, the acceptance letter waiting in my desk at school; I'd told my parents I'd already replied. I imagined what they would say if I told them about Brazil. *"Hai bhagwan!"* my mother would say, clutching her chest, and my father, staring back at me with a bewildered look in his eyes, would say nothing at all.

Two weeks later, on a warm spring day, Jordan and I were in the parking lot when Brendan Simmons called out to us from behind.

"Samir the queer. Is this your boyfriend?"

"Just ignore them," I said.

There were five of them, dressed in baggy T-shirts with horses or alligators stitched on their chests. They crowded around us when Jordan reached for my hand. I was stunned—we had never been physically demonstrative in public—but he held on to it. Firmly.

"Look at this," Brendan said, laughing. "They're holding hands like a couple of fairies."

"Fags," someone said.

"Fruitcakes."

"Queers!"

They laughed.

"You disgust me, you know that?" Brendan said. He walked up to both of us and folded his arms, but his eyes were focused on *me*. "You little sand nigger. You're garbage. Dirt even. The Dumpster's too good for you."

He threw his head back and spit a cold wad of mucus onto my shirt. I recoiled, screaming like a girl, wiping it off with the corner of my sleeve. Brendan and his friends erupted in peals of laughter, pointing at me. So absorbed in my task was I that I hardly noticed Jordan rush out from behind me and punch Brendan in the face.

I froze. Brendan fell backward, blood, thick as molasses, oozing from his nose.

"What the fuck?" someone said. But no one moved. They were staring at Jordan, who was wringing his hand and pacing the parking lot like an ornery cat. He grabbed me by my arm, towing me away. He turned and kicked Brendan in the shin. "Fuck you," he said, glowering, before leading us back to my car.

Later that afternoon, after dropping Jordan home, I pulled in to my driveway and found Lisa standing in front of our garage, crying.

"What is it?" I said, getting out of the car. "What's wrong?"

"It's your father."

"What about him?"

"He's gone."

I led her into the house. We sat down on a suede couch. Lisa crossed her legs. She wore a rose-colored blouse over white silk shorts; her legs were tanned and smooth. Even with tears in her eyes she was beautiful. "Did he tell you where he was going? Did he leave a clue?"

She shook her head. I handed her a tissue and she blotted her cheek. I waited for her to say something. My mother was out running errands, and I wondered if Lisa had known this, if she had waited until my mother's white Audi flicked by her window before getting into her car. She pressed the fabric of her shorts to smooth away a few wrinkles. "He needed time," she said. "He needed to get away." I asked her what had happened. She broke into a sob.

They'd had a fight, the particulars of which were vague; my father had been missing for two days. I pictured him in a hotel room somewhere, drinking Jim Beam. He had done the same thing to my mother years before. Perhaps he had gone to Bloomingdale or Itasca or another small civilization miles away from our town, staying up until late, watching HBO. The sun shone through the windows and highlighted the peach coloring of Lisa's skin, the blond fuzz on her arms. I reached for her hand. "Give it time," I said. "He'll come around." I had said this same thing to my mother, and she had slapped me, telling me to mind my own business. Lisa gave me a hug. Her skin felt like silk. She kissed me on the cheek before heading toward the door. Then she slipped into her red Toyota and waved to me as she disappeared down the road, a trail of exhaust in her wake. Later that evening, when my mother found out the news, she said it was a miracle: finally, after all these years, God had answered her prayers.

We called my father's office. We drove to his favorite restaurants. We asked around at the golf course, too. There was no sign of him. My mother seemed unworried. Lisa stayed away. She was no longer in the front yard, tending to the flowers, or by the mailbox, retrieving the mail, or on the narrow pathways in our neighborhood, going for a jog. She didn't answer the front door when I knocked on it, either. It was a mystery. Then one morning, I drove past my father's house to find his black Jaguar parked by the curb, Lisa's Toyota in the driveway, the rhododendrons flattened, desecrated across the yard.

The relationship resumed. I had expected some sort of cataclysmic ending, the kind my mother and father had had, but Lisa remained, though I saw very little of her. She no longer waved to me from the front yard or invited me in for a snack. When my father barbecued for me on Saturday nights, Lisa remained indoors, on the phone or in front of the computer, in her bedroom for hours on end. Sometimes she didn't come out at all, claiming to be nauseous. I assumed she was punishing me, that I was his scapegoat.

My mother had different theories.

"She's embarrassed," she said, one day in the kitchen. "She's weak and embarrassed and now she is living in her karma. I bet you there's someone else. I bet you he's seeing someone else."

The prospect of another woman fueled my mother's indignation, appeasing her at the same time. I watched her thrive with these new developments. Vast amounts of her time were spent on the phone with her sisters, reporting my father's daily activities.

"I saw him in the backyard today," she would say. "He was alone. She doesn't even sit with him anymore."

If I went over to his house for dinner or to watch TV, my mother would grill me afterward.

"Was Lisa there?" she would ask, her eyes flickering. "Did she talk to you?"

If I said no, that she had spent the majority of her time in her bedroom, my mother would be pleased, smiling inwardly. But if I told her that Lisa had sat with me through *The Wiz,* that she had sung along to the songs, that we had gone for ice cream later and that Lisa had made me laugh, she would be furious, banging dishes, slamming doors.

I started ignoring her again. I spent my evenings with Jordan. We went to the park and lay flat on the merry-go-round and passed a fifth of vodka between our lips. We looked up at the stars and talked about our futures, the people we would be, the places we would go. By that point, I had accepted my admission to Brown, and I started planning the weekends I would visit Jordan before he left for Brazil, the holidays after, when I would fly overseas. He showed me pictures of the landscape and architecture and beaches and cliffs. He said things like, "When you visit me, I'll take you here," or "Maybe I'll convince you to stay forever." We lived through the lives of our future selves, passing our remaining days in a fugue. The semester was winding down and the summer lay ahead of us like a mirage, promising long afternoons by the pool, humid nights in the park, sun-soaked mornings in bed. On our last night of school, Jordan reached into his backpack and pulled out a condom, asking me if I was ready, and though I wasn't, though it would be years before I ever was, I couldn't imagine a more appropriate time to lie.

Three days before graduation, we had our last dance class. The days had grown long, full of deep, lilac sunsets. There was a fervent energy in the air. I was looking forward to spending the whole summer with Jordan. We walked into the dance studio and found Anton waiting for us at the center of the room, a boom box behind him, a smile on his face.

"I want to try something different today," he said. "I want you all to dance freestyle, with no direction."

None of us moved. Anton walked over to the boom box and popped in a CD. He selected a song: "Smooth Criminal." Then he pointed at me. "You, Mr. Jackson. I want to see you dance." I was startled, aware of the many heads turned in my direction, the canned beat bouncing off the walls. I stood in place.

"Well?" he said. "What are you waiting for?"

He squared off a space for me at the center of the room, and I made my way toward it, aware of my reflection in the mirror, the blank stares behind me. I moved, slowly, from side to side. I thought about all the times I had danced like this in my bedroom, my mother standing just outside. I closed my eyes. I opened them and moved faster. The classroom cheered and started singing along to the words. But I could no longer hear them. I was aware only of the sound of my heart, the beat of the drums, the melody in my head. The music stopped and Jordan reached for my hand, leading me outside. We ran across the parking lot under a canopy of stars. There was a playground beyond the parking lot where students went to drink or smoke or kiss behind the slide and it was there that we found them, gathering by the swings.

"Samir the queer."

There were five of them altogether. Brendan was in the lead. The others stood behind him, forming a human wall. "And the boyfriend." Brendan's face was obscured by the dark. A cigarette sparked at his lips. He tossed the cigarette aside and charged at us. I screamed. If they saw me standing there, if they noticed me at all, they didn't show it. It was Jordan they wanted. It was Jordan they dragged across the mud. It was Jordan they towed to the merry-go-round and pummeled in the face. It was Jordan they took turns kicking and punching, kicking and punching, until blood burst like lava from his lips and his nose. I begged them to stop. I threw rocks at their heads. I ran over to Jordan and pulled him by his leg. But it didn't work. I started praying: Hare Rama, Hare Krishna, Hare Rama, Hare Krishna, Hare Rama, Hare Krishna, until a white car pulled in to the parking lot with its headlights on. The crowd dispersed. Brendan ran away. The car turned around. It zipped down the road in the opposite direction, as if it were needed somewhere else. I held my breath, reaching for Jordan's hand, wiping the blood that had collected under his nose and on his chin. He was unrecognizable, pink and bloody like a piece of uncooked steak. He touched my face and his hand felt like sandpaper against my skin. I closed my eyes, afraid that one of the other boys would return to finish off what they had started, but no one did. I could still hear the prayer echoing in my head when Jordan rose to his feet, spitting out some blood, and later, in his driveway, when I carried him into his house.

In the end, my mother was right: Lisa and my father split up. This time it was because of an Indian woman named Kalindi. I was surprised, not that my father would stray, but that he would find a woman exactly like my mother to take Lisa's place. Lisa moved out of my father's house and disappeared from our lives altogether. My mother forgave her. She forgave my father, too, and, three weeks before I left for college, on a dark and gloomy afternoon, he moved back into our house. I was not surprised: I had learned enough to know that life was like a strong current, sweeping you in whichever direction it chose.

One evening, I was emptying the trash in my father's office when a torn letter surfaced, wrinkled and smudged. It was addressed to my mother. It was from Lisa. It said that she'd been pregnant. At least that's what she claimed, among other things: that my father had forced her to get an abortion, that he had threatened to leave if she didn't, and that it was *he* who had pursued *her* in the first place—not the other way around. I remembered the evenings when Lisa would remain indoors, claiming to be nauseous. I wondered if she had been pregnant then. According to her letter, Lisa had tried to get my father to reconcile with my mother, that it was my father who had gone looking for her the moment she was back in town. I didn't know whether to believe this or not. I was not supposed to know these things at all. I waited for a fight that never happened, listening through the walls, perking up whenever my mother slammed a door in the kitchen or raised her voice in the hall. Then one day, I walked into the kitchen with the mail in my hands when my father accosted me from behind, snatching the mail from my grasp, and I knew, by the grave look in his eyes, that everything Lisa had written was true.

I never made it to Brazil. Weeks later, after his bruises had healed, Jordan and I broke up. That night on the playground had withered whatever had grown between us, turning it ugly and vague, until we no longer remembered what had drawn us to each other in the first place. I suppose, in the end, we were afraid. I went away to Brown and he went away to some far corner of the world. Every now and then I got a picture from Jordan in the mail, some smiling image of himself in front of a temple, or on a beach, or climbing the steps of a monument, or swinging from a tree, but soon, even those stopped coming, and eventually, I learned to stop expecting them.

Looking back on it, I realize that my experience with Jordan was just a phase, an initiation, an access point through which I entered a new world. I learned how to love and be loved in ways my parents had never taught me before, and, by the time I was in my thirties, I'd had my heart broken three more times.

My mother was there through it all. She stopped feigning oblivion; eventually she grew to understand my inherent differences, and even to accept them. She was there for me when one man broke my heart after the next, giving me sound advice. She was less cynical, too, though she still continued to pray for us each morning: for my father, for me, and, I suspect, for some greater understanding of the world. ♦

hey, loser

We were friends—Eun-ji and I—in the way you were friends with people you hadn't slept with. That is to say, I really wanted to sleep with her. I got a boner just thinking about it. Sometimes I got a boner thinking about the boner from before. Once, I got a boner thinking about all the other boners I'd had in my lifetime, and how they didn't even compare. I was a wreck. I sat next to her in Anatomy and pretended we were at an opera: the podium a stage, the professor a nymph, Eun-ji reaching for my hand during the final act. Then one day, she invited me over.

"I'm stressed—are you stressed? We should study together or something."

I spent the rest of the afternoon preparing myself, cutting my hair, trimming my beard, buying a new deodorant because I had begun to cultivate a smell. I shaved my body in places I had never shaved before—or even seen. I didn't have condoms, so I stopped at the free clinic and stuffed my pockets with a handful. Then I went home, showered, dried, put on jeans and a shirt. I was ready.

Eun-ji answered the door wearing sweatpants.

"Oh," she said. "Have you been out?"

Her apartment was nicer than mine, with plush white carpeting, soft cream walls, pictures of kittens placed all over the bookshelf and bar. I told her I loved it. She said it was just okay. We were sitting in her bedroom, spreading our textbooks over the floor in front of us, when Eun-ji turned to me and smiled.

"We can *do it* if you want; just don't get it on my sheets."

We started kissing—quick, darting kisses that were like the brush of a moth's wings. After it was over, we sat around staring at the floor.

"Well," she said, quietly, "that was different."

It happened again, after the final, and once more, before winter break. The streets were covered with hard glittering frost when Eun-ji reached for my hand.

"I like you, Raj."

We went to coffee houses and bars, traded secrets in the dark, told each other things we had never told anyone before: the time I went to summer camp and got a blow job from the counselor, the time I cheated on my physics final. The time I attempted suicide by taking a bottle of pills—it was my senior year of college, and my girlfriend had stopped returning my calls.

"I didn't mean to do it," I said. "I just wanted her to call me back."

Eun-ji kissed me, offering stories of her own—like the time she got drunk in Chicago and woke up in a strange apartment in Kenosha, sixty miles away. She described the harrowing journey home: the clogged traffic, the circling birds, the pregnancy test she hid from her roommate, which was positive, and which she dealt with swiftly, never saying a word. I held her hand and kissed every goose bump and mole.

We were inseparable. Long afternoons were spent walking

hand in hand, from class to class, studying in the library, stealing a touch or a kiss. Final exams were approaching, but I couldn't focus on a single word. I was transfixed by her: the way she held her highlighter, the way she flicked her hair, the plastic sheen of her creamy white skin. The things that fell out of her bag: pink cookies and a box of red bean jelly her parents had brought back from Korea, which she plucked surreptitiously between her manicured nails. Sometimes she looked up at me and frowned.

"Are you even studying?"

"Of course I am."

"I'm worried about you, Raj."

"I'm fine."

I wasn't. Each hour that passed brought me closer to the realization that winter break was approaching, that we could be separated for weeks. That I could be forgotten, forsaken, cast aside like yesterday's news. On our last night together, Eun-ji made pasta primavera and straddled me on her bed. Then she was gone.

I went home and sulked for days. I tossed and turned in my bed. Eun-ji was in St. Lucia, posting pictures from the beach. My parents wanted to watch movies and I wanted to track her every move on Facebook. Friday night: dinner with family! Saturday morning: jog on the beach! Saturday night: all dressed up for drinks! In each picture her face was bright with exertion and her hair, slicked down or scraped back into a bun, was the color of damp earth. One night she called me. It was late. The house was dark. My cell phone vibrated on the pillow next to my head.

"I want you, Raj," she said, breathlessly. "Oh, god. I wish you were here."

I told her I wanted her, too. It was like that for a while. We sent messages back and forth, promising to meet as soon as she was back; toward the end of break, we did, at a condo her parents had rented for the season. It was there that I told her I loved her. She said we needed to talk.

"I like you, Raj—don't get me wrong—but things are moving a little fast."

"What do you mean?"

"I mean we barely know each other, and already you're saying these things."

"What things—that I love you?" My heart dropped. "But it's true. I love you more than anything in the world!"

"Oh, Raj."

It was over; she needed a break. The semester was starting up again and she needed to concentrate on school. Maybe I should do the same. I didn't tell her the truth: that I was failing. I'd received a letter that afternoon. My parents had asked me how my first year of medical school was going, and I'd said I got all As.

I was used to getting As, though. In high school, my name—Rajesh Desai—was perched precisely above Matthew Desilva's on the school honor roll. In college, I breezed through the courses, spending most of my time at bars. The summer after graduation was one of my brightest. I went to Europe, backpacking through Spain, screwing dark-haired women in even darker hotels. I returned in August and my parents insisted I stay home: *This is our time together.* But I moved in early, two weeks before class, and when they offered to come with me I refused, telling them I could do it on my own. I spent a weekend familiarizing myself with the campus. I bought my textbooks ahead of time. I took notes in anticipation of the work we would be slapped with: the dissections and lectures and exams. I took notes of my notes, using sticky tabs and markers and pens. I went to the library and sat there until five in the morning, until a peach color proliferated across the sky. Then something strange happened.

I'm not sure what it was. I don't know when it disappeared: the will. I suspect it had something to do with love, but what exactly? Before Eun-ji, I was dedicated, diligent, never missing a day of class. I was so engrossed in my studies that I hardly noticed her sitting in front of me each day. Then one day, I did. It was like a light flicked on inside of me. Instead of listening to the lecturer I would imagine the two of us on a beach, at a cocktail party, or a hospital even, Eun-ji delivering our firstborn. It was maddening.

When I returned to school, the campus was blanketed in snow; the trees were stripped bare. The radiator was broken in my apartment, so I spent my evenings wrapped up in a comforter, drinking Jim Beam. Our classes resumed, but I couldn't bear the thought of seeing Eun-ji freshly tanned from St. Lucia, talking to her friends. So I stayed home.

I started tracking her on Facebook again. On Monday she was at the gym. On Wednesday she was at a café. On Friday she went out with her friends, posting pictures of herself from a bar. There she was in a black tube top, gold glitter on her eyes. There was a man standing next to her.

He was tagged.

His name was Michael Gray. He was a law student (I knew this because I had clicked on his page). He was political, posting links to various injustices happening all over the world. Sometimes he posted a gif of a cat, or a snapshot of the American flag. He was opinionated, arguing passionately against the Supreme Court's decision to legalize gay marriage, going on to say that there were more important things to worry about than the rights of gays. Much of his news feed consisted of articles on immigration and health care and guns. He seemed like the sort of white guy who was passively racist, which made his interest in Eun-ji all the more confusing. Once, he commented on a video of a black man being gunned down by the cops: "How are we supposed to believe he wasn't armed?"

He was pompous—his page was plastered with pictures of his bulging muscles, his varnished face, his collection of watches and neckties and shoes. He wore his ash blond hair cropped close to his scalp, which was pink in the summertime, glistening like a piece of cooked Spam. I switched off my computer and passed out in my bed.

The next morning, there was another picture: he and Eun-ji were holding hands outside an IHOP. I looked at others, dating back to high school. There they were on a beach, on a swing, in Prague, on a cobblestone road. There were comments, glorious comments filling up the spaces beneath it, posted by family members and friends. I couldn't wrap my head around it. I couldn't believe what I was seeing. I called her on the phone. "Who is he?"

"Huh?"

It was dawn; soft light slinked in through the blinds. Eun-ji was sleepy, yawning into the receiver.

"Who, Eun-ji?"

She was silent.

"Answer me."

Nothing.

"Were you fucking him the whole time?"

She hung up the phone.

I called three more times; she didn't answer. I sent text messages; she didn't reply. I wrote a three-page email outlining our entire relationship—the lows and the highs—then I walked to class. The wind was like a cold slap against my face. The frost bit into my fingers. The sharp air sliced through my lungs. Classes were canceled so I walked back home, removing my scarf and my shoes, my jacket limp with snow. Outside, students scraped windshields and laughed. A fat woman slipped on the ice. A salt truck rumbled past my window. I opened my laptop and found a message on Facebook. It was from Michael Gray. It said, "Hey, loser. Leave my girlfriend alone."

The words pinged in my mind for hours. *Hey, loser.* I heard them while washing my hair, or making a sandwich, or reading a novel. I heard them after the first beer and the second beer and the third. Ping! Ping! Ping! Finally, I opened my laptop and replied.

I checked in the morning to see if he had responded, and later in the afternoon. Nothing. The blizzard cleared. The sidewalks emerged. Melted snow rushed through the metal grates in the road. Classes resumed and my professor emailed me, asking me where I was. I said I had the flu. In a way, I did.

I awoke two days later, feeling renewed. I walked into class with an extra bounce in my step. I took a seat in the first row and opened my textbook to the first page, when I felt Eun-ji's presence behind me, staring at the back of my head.

My grades improved. I passed one test and then another, asking questions after class, spending hours in the medical library poring over my notes. On weekends I discussed hospital politics over a pint of beer. Sometimes Eun-ji would be there, stealing glances in my direction. She stopped being a presence in my mind. It was funny how love could do that: plant roots in your heart like a tenant who won't leave and then, just like that, they're gone.

Then one morning, she tapped me on my shoulder.

"Hey."

She had gained some weight. Her thighs swelled in her jeans. She asked me if I wanted to grab a coffee, but I shook my head. "I don't think that's a good idea."

"Why not?"

"Because it isn't."

There was panic in her eyes. She stormed out of the room. The next morning, I took my seat in the front of class and opened my notebook to a fresh page. I felt her eyes on the back of my head. After class was over, she hurried to catch up to me, but I quickened my pace. It went on like that for a while. I watched her squirm. Every now and then, I caught her frowning at the chalkboard ahead, looking miserable. Soon, she started dressing up as if for my benefit—short skirts and cropped blouses that stretched over the swell of her breasts. She wore more makeup than I preferred. Sometimes she showed up at parties and flirted loudly with other boys. Once, she caught up to me just as I was walking into Anatomy lab, grabbing me by the shoulder, asking me again.

This time I said yes.

"I thought Michael and I could work," she said. "I needed to give it time."

"And now?"

"And now it's done."

We made love in her bed, on her desk, in the library, after studying for an exam. Her breasts were like pillows of dough and her ass was like a mold of gelatin, wiggling with each step. I grabbed each part as if it were my own. Winter turned to spring. Torrential rains pelted the earth. These were the best moments, when we lay in bed listening to the persistent crackle of a storm. Sometimes we stared at the blurred lights outside her window and it was like we were the only two people in the world. For spring break, Eun-ji invited me to her parents' time-share in Aruba. We spent the entire weekend baking in the sun.

I started keeping things at her place—razors and combs, underwear and socks, the tattered novels I read from time to time. The printed pictures of our trip to Aruba, which I had posted on Facebook already, so that everyone would know. Once, after an exam, we went to a bar. It was our first shelf of the year. Everyone was wired. Eun-ji was wearing a strapless black dress. Her arms were tanned apart from the pale imprints her bathing suit had left behind. We were fresh from lovemaking, ordering drinks at the bar, when I felt a hand on my shoulder. I spun around.

I hadn't expected to see him in person; the law campus was nowhere near ours—though we shared the same bars, the same dorms, the same restaurants smoky with lamb kebabs, the same stretch of green pasture that connected the graduate campus to the undergraduate one. I remembered the message I'd sent him months ago—*Fuck you, motherfucker*—and felt the urge to laugh. Michael brought his face close to mine, revealing a jagged white smile.

"Got a problem?"

He was massive—a few inches taller than me and wider, too, with strong shoulders and thick arms. His skin was the color of a ripe tomato. His eyes flashed sharply like the tip of a blade.

"No," I said, feeling the weight of his grip. "Not at all."

He laughed, pushing me against the bar. I fell backward. He pushed me again. I straightened myself and reached for my wallet, offering him a beer.

"Look, man, I don't want to fight you."

"Are you trying to be a smart-ass?"

"What?"

"Do you think I can't buy my own beer?"

"Not at all."

"Do you think I don't know what's going on? That I don't know what you're trying to do? Do you think I'm some kind of idiot?"

I said nothing.

"I don't know where *you're* from, bud, but in *this* country we have a little thing called respect."

He was drunk; I could smell it on his breath. Sweat gathered on his forehead like beads of fat on a ham. I raised my palms, thinking this would appease him, but he kneed me in the groin. I cried out in pain. He drew his fist back to punch me when a small voice bleated from the back of the crowd.

"Let him go, Mikey."

It was Eun-ji, back with a fresh drink in her hand. She grabbed Michael by his arm and he went limp. She whispered something in his ear and he let go of my neck. He walked away. I was spared. Except for the injured voice knocking around in my skull.

"Fuck you," I said.

He stopped in his tracks. "Excuse me?"

"You heard me. I said, fuck you."

He narrowed his eyes, looking me up and down.

"Fuck you, motherfucker," I said, louder this time. "Fuck you. Fuck you. Fuck you. I *do* think you're an idiot, actually. I bet you're even dumber than you fucking look!"

The light went out of my head, and with it, the entire universe, the dim glow of the bar, the music and dancing and rhapsodic jeers. I woke with a throbbing pain in my face. Eun-ji was kneeling, ministering to my wounds, but not before stealing one last look in Michael Gray's direction. Something clouded in her eyes. Later that evening—and every evening after that—she would tell me it was nothing; I was crazy.

But I knew that it was there.

We didn't make love much that week, or the week after that, and when we did, it was tepid, Eun-ji turning her head.

"It's him," I'd say. "I know it. It's him."

"Don't be ridiculous. I'm right here."

She would finish quickly, closing her eyes. I would ask if I was coming over later and she would say, "It's up to you." Once, we went an entire day without speaking. I started drinking again—beer and wine in the mornings and a glass of Jim Beam before bed. I went on Facebook to see what she was doing. The last picture was of us on the beach in Aruba, smiling under the sun. Suddenly, in class, she hesitated before taking the seat next to mine. At the library, she closed her books before announcing an incipient cold. Once, she stopped in the middle of our lovemaking just to answer the phone. "Who was it?" I said, freeing a strand of her hair that was clinging to her skin.

She said it was no one.

A month passed. I went to the mall, sampling perfumes, lotions, gourmet chocolates flecked with salt. I wrapped everything up with a bottle of wine. I wrote a letter about how special it was for two people to find each other in a world full of billions, defying all odds. Then I knocked on her door. She didn't answer. I knocked again. A light went on inside. A pair of shoes scraped the floor before the door opened, slowly, revealing a sliver of Eun-ji's face.

"Surprise," I said. "It's an early birthday present."

I leaned in to kiss her, but she turned her head. I reached for her hand, but she pulled it away.

"Is everything okay?" I said, though I knew, then, that it wasn't.

"I wish you would have called, Raj. You can't just show up here unannounced."

"Why not?"

"Because you can't."

"But I love you."

She lowered her gaze.

"Say it," I said, stepping forward. "Say you love me."

I was aware of how ridiculous this all looked, how unnecessary I had now become. But there was no turning back.

"Say it."

"Raj . . ."

"I want you to say it."

I grabbed her by the arm this time, squeezing it tight.

"I think you should go."

"Why?" I said, shouting. "Give me one goddamn reason why."

She slammed the door in my face. I marched across the street and opened the bottle of wine. I remained in the shadows, waiting for something to happen. Anything. Then the door swung open; Michael Gray emerged. I hurled the bottle of wine. It somersaulted across the sky. Eun-ji came running out of the apartment, screaming at the top of her lungs.

It was over. I asked Eun-ji if we could be friends—I couldn't bear the thought of losing her forever—but she said we were never friends to begin with, that that was the problem. It was funny how love could do that: give a person amnesia. A few days later, she was back with Michael Gray. I saw them on the quad together, holding hands. He attended our medical school events and I suspect she attended his law ones. They were a real couple, an example to the rest of our class, and I was just the idiot who got in the way. That was how the story would go. There would be no mention of the bottle of wine that shattered against the doorframe and flung a piece of glass that pierced Michael Gray's cornea, causing him to wear a patch for the rest of the year.

During my final year of school, I was living in a house with some friends when I walked outside to find that my tires had been slashed. A sick joke, I was told, some freshman's idea of a prank, but I wondered. When I found toilet paper strewn over our front yard, I was told the house across the street had also been tagged. When egg whites formed a milky crust over the windows, I was pointed in the direction of the sorority house, two blocks over, where eggshells littered the lawn.

I graduated from medical school. I framed my diploma. I posed for pictures in my cap and gown. I moved to Los Angeles, where I applied for and was accepted into a cardiology program at UCLA. It was there, on a bright summer afternoon, after a happy hour with friends, that I met her: Mona Singh.

She was a NICU fellow. She was Punjabi. She had long sleek hair that fell past her waist. At parties she wore blue eye shadow and dark lipstick the color of plums. We went for hikes in the park, drives up the coast, cocktails in dark restaurants or dive bars or clubs. We shucked oysters under a netting of stars, listening to the soft spatter of ocean waves. Mona lived in a fancy condo, with white lacquered tiles. I lived in a studio with a white refrigerator.

Her parents were jewelers in Bel-Air. On weekends I accompanied her home. Mona's mother skewered kebabs and her father opened a bottle of wine, and together, we looked up at the stars and thought about how the air had never felt purer, the moon had never looked brighter, how the night had never been as magical as that one, right there, in her parents' backyard.

On Sundays we shared sections of the paper and listened to music and Mona made blood orange mimosas and we drank them by the pool. Her parents prepared a room for me on the other side of the house, but at night, after everyone had fallen asleep, I snuck over into Mona's room. She would be waiting for me with a smile on her face, her blouse wide open, her nipples stiff as stones. One night, she was staring into the blue glow of her computer screen when she turned around and smiled.

"Who's Eun-ji?"

She spun the monitor around so that I saw Eun-ji and me on Facebook, holding hands, a stolen moment, captured among friends. I hadn't seen her in years, though I'd often clicked on her page. Sometimes I'd type up a tearful message I had neither the inspiration nor the courage to send. Once, I'd dialed her number in the middle of the night, just to listen to the sound of her voice. But that was the past, before I'd met Mona, before my life had changed in ways I never imagined they could. Now, she was nothing more than a fork in the road, a ding in my bumper, a vague image in my rearview mirror, fading away.

We were married a year later, at a Hilton hotel. Mona wore a red sari. I rode in on a horse. Her parents sprang for a trip to Bora Bora: first class. We stayed in a hut overlooking a glassy lagoon. We sunbathed and snorkeled and ran laps on the beach. We ate lobster and swordfish and extracted tender meat from crabs, and, when it was all over we returned to a three-bedroom town house in Silver Lake, overlooking the hills. Mona flipped through magazines, ordering sofas, armchairs, crystal-studded lamps, a gilded mirror that was tall enough to touch the ceiling and that we kept at an angle against the wall. She filled the space with her things: her dresses and shoes, her nighties and robes, the hair-brushes that grew matted and dense with each use. I awoke to the scent of her shampoo as she slipped in and out of the bathroom, fastening her earrings or polishing her shoes. We worked at the same hospital, joined the same gym. On Sundays we went hiking and got drunk off gin fizz. Then we rushed home, our hands traveling to the places we had long known, the freckles and blemishes and moles, the hollows we'd kissed a thousand times before. It was the life I had always wanted, the life I had always dreamt of, and then, just like that, it was gone.

His name was Landon, and he was her trainer. He had the kind of reasonable smile that made you want to punch him in his face, which I did, naturally, after finding out the news. Discovering it, really. It happened on a Sunday. Mona had come home from the gym. I was in the living room, watching TV, when she dropped her handbag on the floor. She went for a shower. I rifled through the bag. To this day, I'm not sure why I did it. Jealousy, maybe; suspicion, sure. But that was it. We were happy. Still, I was aware of what people said. I'd heard the whispers during work. I was there, one Friday evening at a hospital charity function, when an electrocardiogram fellow made a comment about Mona's breasts. I nearly punched him in the face. But I never thought it would come to this. I found the receipt buried under a pile of her things—tampons, tissues, lipsticks, creams—and smoothed it out over my lap. There was only one item listed: a box of condoms. Mona was on the pill. I threw the bag across the room. I waited for her to emerge from the shower, wet hair clinging to her face, before confronting her in the hall.

"Who is he?"

"Huh?"

"Condoms, Mona. Who are you buying condoms for?"

I held up the receipt.

She started to cry. "It was a mistake," she kept saying, over and over again, into her hands.

But I was no longer listening.

My therapist said I blacked out. He said it was common. He said it happened during moments of high stress; that, given the circumstances, anyone could have reacted the same way. But I didn't believe him. I don't know how I ended up at the gym with a dumbbell in my hands, a trail of havoc in my wake: broken dishes, splattered walls, scratch marks on Mona's Mercedes, a pool of spilled red wine. All I know is, I was standing over Landon's crumpled-up body with a ten-pounder in my hands, waving it around like a buffoon. I looked at my reflection in the mirror.

I couldn't tell you who was looking back.

According to my therapist, this was all very normal. He said I was having an *existential crisis*. He said I needed time, that I should come up with an alternative method of coping, a fantasy world in which everything was reasonable and calm. Visualize it, he said. Imagine that you're there. Eventually, everything around you will disappear.

It didn't.

Mona left me, and I had to get a lawyer. I found the advertisement online. M.G. & Associates: defense attorneys extraordinaire. Their office was in a reflective building downtown. In the stone lobby, glass elevators floated up and down like balloons. A perfumed receptionist looked up from her desk.

"Law offices?" she said, lazily. "Third floor."

I was nervous; I had never been in trouble with the law before. I adjusted my suit and stared at my reflection in the mirror. My eyes were bloodshot. My skin was pale. My face was swollen from all the medication: Xanax and some little white pills I'd started popping like M&M's. It was hot outside, ninety, ninety-five by my guess, and the air-conditioning froze the sweat right off my skin. I went over my story a few times before the elevator doors opened, swiftly, revealing a square of pale light.

He was standing by the reception area in a three-piece suit. It was him, all right. There was no mistaking it. I was terrified by the sheer coincidence of it all, the sudden intersection of our lives, and yet, in some small, strange way, I had expected it all along. I stared at the placard and eventually it became clear: M.G. & Associates.

Michael Gray.

He hadn't changed much. His pink skin still shone like a scab. The ash blond hair was still shorn to his scalp. He looked garish in white pinstripes and a bright pink tie. He smiled at a woman, a client perhaps, before leading her toward the door, at which point our eyes met.

I should have appealed to him. I should have shaken his hand. I should have thrown my shoulders back and remarked on what a wonderful surprise this all was, how, when you really thought about it, we were just a couple of ignorant kids. But I bolted instead, past the elevators, down the stairs, into the lobby, and, just as my legs were about to give out, into the parking lot beyond. The last thing I remembered was Michael's mouth hanging open in consternation, in terror even, as if it were he—not I—who was afraid.

Later that evening, I logged on to Facebook. I clicked on her page. The engagement in Chicago, the wedding in New York, three children (two boys and a girl, all with Eun-ji's creamy white skin). Her husband was a heart surgeon named Dominic. He ran marathons and races in which you swam through mud. I scrolled through the history that had once united and divided us, tearing us apart, looking for some signs of Michael's exit. But there were none. Then I found the picture. The one Mona had pointed out to me in her room.

She wore a lemon-colored coat; her hands were in gloves. We were standing outside a bar we used to go to called Dudley's. The rest of our class was there, too, making silly faces. I read the comments, lengthy exultations about what a wonderful time it had been, before leaving one of my own.

All night long, I dreamt of an alternate future, a fantasy world in which Eun-ji and I were friends, in which our Facebook contact became real contact and our likes became love. The next morning, I logged on to Facebook and checked if she had replied, if the comment was still there.

But it was gone—deleted. I closed my laptop and went back to bed, shutting my eyes.

Then I opened them, swiftly.

The message was waiting for me at the bottom of the screen: "Hi."

I clicked on the window and began typing up a response, my heart hammering in my chest, my fingers splayed over the keys. I fired it off. I took a deep breath. I poured myself a drink in the kitchen and waited—seconds, minutes, hours, years—but I never heard from her again. ♦

just a friend

Every now and then, I asked Ashwin about his wife: in line at the movies, or after a beer.

Or after we'd screwed.

He would reach over and take the cigarette from my hands, kissing my smoky mouth. Then he would change the subject. I never believed for a minute they were intimate. I never believed he was in love.

I'd met him at a gay bar. He was shy and even a little rude when I walked over to him and introduced myself, shaking his hand, and later, when he'd rejected me, going home with someone else.

I wanted him then and there.

I didn't have him until three weeks later, when he called me out of the blue. I didn't even remember his name. He asked to speak to Jonathan and I told him my name was John. Then he asked if we could meet.

"I'm sorry, who is this?"

"Ashwin Acharya."

"And we met where?"

"At the Babylon nightclub, three Saturdays ago."

I remembered him: tall and handsome, with a shock of dark brown hair. He'd worn a pink ascot and expensive-looking shoes; he was alone. I was in my tank top and jeans. I remembered laughing at him, thinking he had taken a wrong turn on his way to the Trump Hotel or something. But he hadn't. He told me this over the phone. He also told me I was cute, and that he liked my blond hair—I didn't tell him it was dyed. Instead, I floated off into a dream world of Arab sheikhs and shopping trips to Dubai; I didn't realize he was Indian at the time. I felt stupid later, making sure to tell him that I loved Indian food—that chicken *makhani* was my favorite—and that Aishwarya Rai was beautiful. He seemed less concerned with this and more concerned with my educational background. I told him the truth: that I had dropped out of college and I was bartending at a restaurant downtown. I was twenty-two.

He was forty-five. I was shocked when he told me. I thought he was thirty or maybe even twenty-something. He had smooth copper skin and bright eyes. He was rich, too, judging from the Mercedes sedan he picked me up in on our first date. He lived in the suburbs of Chicago. He had driven forty minutes just to see me.

"Where should we go?" he asked.

"I thought you would know."

He took me to a restaurant on the fringes of town. I figured it was a place he visited regularly but later realized it was because he didn't want to be seen. He told me this in a motel room, off the freeway, after we'd screwed.

"So you like sleeping with men?" I said.

Earlier that evening, I'd asked Ashwin if he had a boyfriend; he'd told me he had a wife. I was disappointed but not surprised.

I'd met men like him before. They had girlfriends or wives and walked freely in two separate worlds, just because they could. They weren't camp like I was. For a moment, I was envious (though whether it was of Ashwin or of his wife, I wasn't sure).

"I like sleeping with *you,*" he said.

I thought that would be the end of it—the way most dates of this nature were—but then two days later he called me again.

"I was thinking about you."

"You were?"

I was standing on the platform of the L, waiting for a train to take me to Wicker Park, where I stayed in a shared apartment to which Ashwin had never been. He was driving home from work. He was a dentist and he owned a practice in Highland Park. I pictured him with his leather gloves and his big black Mercedes, pulling out of a parking space or a garage. I wondered about his house—I pictured a large mansion with pretty moldings. I wondered if he had kids. I asked him this on our second date.

"Not yet."

I was surprised. I'd assumed someone his age would have at least one. My expression must have betrayed this, because later he explained to me that his wife was very young.

"How young?"

He paused. We were sitting at a bar near my apartment, with frosted glass windows. He reached for my hand.

"Let's not talk about it."

We began seeing each other twice a week, sometimes on weekends, staying in motel rooms and, when he was comfortable, in my room. My roommate was never home. Her name was Stephanie, and she was dating some tech guy who lived in River North. When Ashwin saw her picture for the first time he was confused.

"Her parents don't mind?"

"Mind what?"

"That she is living with a man."

I laughed. "I'm gay," I said.

"Her parents know you are gay?"

"Of course," I replied. "Everyone does."

He looked disappointed by this, as if there was something undignified about it. Then he glanced around the room. He found it charming, with its mismatched furniture, its multicolored walls, its unopened bottles of discounted wine. He was bold, touching things at random and not caring whose they were. We would order in or go out to eat or else watch a movie in my bed, cuddling up after sex. He was competent in that area—he would pin me down and whisper something sexy in my ear, something sweet even, like he couldn't get enough of me, or he never wanted to stop. Then he would pin my hands behind my back and pull on my hair. Unlike most guys he would stay long after it was over, smoking a cigarette or else nibbling on whatever we had eaten that day: Chinese noodles, linguine with clams, chicken salad sandwiches from the restaurant down the road. He was the youngest of four children. He had immigrated in his twenties. I asked him what it was like back home and he told me it didn't matter.

Only it did matter. It mattered to *me*. I started to wonder about his life at home, about his wife, Uma, who, according to Ashwin, was closer to my age than his own. He said that prior to their wedding they had never even met; he was thirty-eight and his parents were concerned. They were getting older. They had diabetes. They had asked him once how he would feel, knowing they had died worrying about him. So he agreed. He married. He never looked back.

I found this all very poignant and sad, but Ashwin didn't seem to care at all. He didn't seem to care about anything, really. Once I asked him—I asked him what he told his wife he was doing when he was sleeping with me.

He smiled.

"She's not here."

"Where is she?"

"In India."

"For how long?"

We were sitting up in bed, watching the news. Ashwin had ordered pizza. He was folding a slice of pepperoni into his mouth.

"She's been there for six weeks," he said.

I did the math in my head; it had been six weeks since Ashwin and I had first met.

"When does she come back?" I asked. He was silent. "When?"

"Not for a while."

I asked him why he never told me this, why he never talked about his wife, why, at the very least, he never invited me to his home. He reached under the covers and smacked me on my thigh.

"You want to see my house?" he said, smiling. "Okay."

He invited me for the weekend. I decided to cook him a meal. I borrowed one of Stephanie's cookbooks and began thumbing through the pages; then I went grocery shopping. It was the first time that Ashwin let me pay for something. I decided on a chicken curry dish with sultanas and steamed rice. I figured he would be surprised: all we ever ate was takeaway.

Ashwin wasn't home. He'd left the keys under a mat along with a note that read: "See you soon." I walked around. There was a wide glass staircase, walnut floors, long gray sofas upholstered in leather and suede. The back of the house overlooked a glittering lake and a strip of forest beyond. There was a boat moored at a dock—a white speedboat with red piping, floating under a cobalt sky.

I had seen houses like this before as a child, when my father took me to work with him on Sunday afternoons. He was an electrician who installed hi-fi systems inside rich people's homes. His clients were mostly doctors or lawyers. They lived in brick houses with circular drives. They had identical children, all with blond hair. Sometimes these blond children would talk to me about the weather in Aruba. I had never been to Aruba, but they talked anyway, their skin tanned, their hair twisted into braids, as if I, too, had been there. Once, in high school, I accompanied my father on an installation at the home of one of my classmates, a popular boy named Dylan Shaw. I didn't realize it was *his* house at the time. I felt embarrassed, standing there in my overalls while my father looked up and down the walls. "Geez Louise," he said, shaking Dylan's hand. "This is some place you got here." Later, at school, I ran into Dylan in the hallway, and when I walked into the men's room he followed me inside.

I unloaded the groceries and opened Stephanie's cookbook, thumbing through the pages again. Then I explored the house, peeking into closets and doors. The living room featured a plasma TV, a stainless steel bar, colorful paintings of octagons and squares. There were elegant touches all over the house: silk pillows and white lacquered tables all gleaming under the sun. It wasn't what I had imagined the home of an Indian person to look like at all—in high school, I'd had a friend named Kareena, and her house was crammed with pictures of elephants and gods. Privately, I had been hoping to see pictures of Ashwin's wife; I had been thinking about her all along. But there were none. I walked into their bedroom. I glanced around. I pulled back the covers of Ashwin's king-size bed. Then I got inside. The windows overlooked the lake, which, by that point, looked like a sheet of smoked glass. Moments later, I heard the garage door open and caught a glimpse of Ashwin's sleek black Mercedes as it glided up the drive. I hurried downstairs.

He was tired but eager, taking me in his arms. He said he had been thinking about me all day.

"It was you that kept me going," he said. "I was thinking about your face."

I tried to picture him in his big bright office, holding a dental instrument in his hands. I remembered my own dentist then: a large man named Dr. Morrison who drove a bottle-green Porsche.

"Study hard, John," he'd said, "and one day this, too, can be yours."

Ashwin wore a dress shirt and tie; he loosened them in the kitchen. His dark hair was slicked back from his face.

"Some wine?" he asked, pouring a little into a crystal glass.

I was struck by how formal it was. At my apartment we drank wine out of plastic cups, huddled under my sheets. My living room was unlivable. Suddenly I longed for the intimacy of it, for the way we clung to each other in the middle of the night. Here, in this expansive space, sitting at opposite ends of a glass dining table, we were far apart.

The wine was delicious. So was the food: gourmet cheese, premade lasagna, a chocolate mousse torte. It would be my turn to cook tomorrow. We stayed up late, talking into the night. Ashwin lit a fire. He told me the house was his long before his wife had arrived, the furniture his choice, the design his conception. I couldn't help but imagine myself living in it. I couldn't help but imagine other things, too: a dog and a child and a car in which to cart them around. I was thinking about these things when Ashwin looked at me from across the table, smiling.

He screwed me on the floor, pressing my face into the rug. Then he opened another bottle of wine. "Like this," he said, swirling it around, explaining that the wine needed to breathe. I felt ignorant in his presence. Ashwin regaled me with his travels—he had been to Cambodia recently, to an ancient city called Angkor, where he had visited the largest Hindu temple in the world. He asked me if I'd ever traveled and I nodded my head.

"To Europe," I lied.

He asked me where and I panicked. I wasn't even sure that I could point to Europe on a map. The only places I had ever been were the amusement parks in Florida and California, when I was a child. "To England," I said.

He had been there three times.

The next morning, I awoke in Ashwin's bed, tangled in his sheets. I'd had too much to drink. I looked over and saw that his side of the bed was already made. I went downstairs. He was rooting around in the kitchen, cooking bacon and eggs. He handed me a fork and a plate. "Good morning," he said.

"What time is it?"

"Ten."

It was the first time I had seen him this way, with his thin legs exposed, his face unshaven. He looked tired.

"I thought we could go out on the boat," he said. "It's warmer today."

I nodded. I drank three cups of water. I felt nauseous. Ashwin gave me some medicine and encouraged me to eat, rubbing the back of my head. When I was feeling better we changed into our clothes—jeans and sweaters and a light jacket Ashwin let me borrow—and headed out onto the dock.

His boat was long and shapely, with tan leather seats. There was an ice chest in the center filled with sandwiches and beer; Ashwin must have packed it before I woke up. He took the wheel.

"Would you like to try it?" he said.

I had never driven a boat before, but I said yes anyway. Then Ashwin grabbed me suddenly and guided me with his hands. I threw the engine in reverse. Ashwin fell forward.

"Oh, god," I said. "Are you okay?"

He didn't say anything for a while, just lay there on the floor like a dead animal. In his silver jacket he looked like one of the silver-skinned fish I had seen washed up on the shore. I was certain he would reprimand me, tell me I was an idiot, that I didn't know what I was doing, that I was too inept for his home. Instead he laughed. He stood up and tossed his head back and laughed and laughed, the sun shining, the lake gleaming, the birds dancing over us like moths over a flame. I went over to kiss him, placing my hands on either side of his face, but he pulled away.

That afternoon, Ashwin made coffee while I set about preparing dinner. I had marked the necessary pages in Stephanie's cookbook—highlighting the portions in which she had indicated to use two chilies instead of one, three tomatoes instead of four, red onions instead of yellow. It said to roast whole fresh spices from scratch instead of using spices from a bag. I had not read this before. Still, I continued, cleaning the chicken and marinating it with yogurt and salt. I chopped onions and fried them with cumin and cloves. I added ginger and garlic, too. The fragrance was intoxicating. I pictured Ashwin and me on a boat in the middle of the Indian Ocean, Ashwin reaching toward me instead of pulling away.

"What's this?" he said, looking over my shoulder. "You're making chicken masala."

I had tried chicken marsala before, at the Olive Garden. I told Ashwin this and he laughed.

"Not marsala," he said. "Masala. It means spice."

I was embarrassed again, and also terrified; Ashwin told me his mother used to make him chicken masala every Sunday night.

"Does Uma make it?" I asked.

I knew it was a mistake as soon as I had said it. But I couldn't help myself. I'd been hoping to find out about her all along. I'd assumed that I would, that, being in her house, among all of her things, I would be impressed by her somehow. But in this glass palace there wasn't a single trace of her, not even her clothes.

"Uma doesn't cook," he said, noticing a stain on the countertop, wiping it cleanly away.

The meal was awful: the chicken was rubbery and the curry tasted like Campbell's Tomato Soup. But Ashwin didn't seem to care. He ate noisily, smacking his lips. After dinner, he suggested we go to a bar—a gay bar called Renaissance. We got dressed in Ashwin's room. I wore a floral-print shirt, acid-washed jeans. Ashwin wore a dress shirt and tie. I laughed at him.

"You can't wear that," I said.

"Why not?"

"Because it's not sexy enough."

I stripped off his clothes. Ashwin flipped me onto the bed and pressed his belly against my back. He said we could bring the nightclub home with us; there was no need to go to a bar. He had a strobe light and a fantastic sound system. He asked me to meet him downstairs. When I arrived, all the lights were off except for two red and white orbs flashing around the room. Ashwin reached for my hand.

He danced well—surprisingly well. I should have known better. I should have remembered the Bollywood movies Kareena and I would watch at her house, how everyone was dancing, how they sometimes held hands. Kareena told me that in India it was common for men to hold hands—it didn't make them queer, it just meant that they were friends. I pictured Ashwin and me in India. I pictured Ashwin holding my hand. I wondered if people would think that *I* was just a friend, too.

Then Ashwin spun me around the room and told me that he had never felt this way before.

"About a man?" I asked.

"About anyone."

I found it utterly romantic. I had always dreamt of something like this. In high school I'd had visions of a life just like this one, with a man just like Aswhin. I'd pictured a house where everything was beautiful and where the pains of adolescence—the bullies, the scars, the look on Dylan Shaw's face when he saw me on his doorstep that morning, and later, in the men's room, after he followed me inside—simply faded away. I'd imagined there was someone out there who could make it all disappear, reinvent me somehow. And now there was.

"Do you love me?" I asked, whispering in Ashwin's ear.

He told me he did.

That night, I dreamt of things I had never experienced before: palm trees and deserts and spices and sounds, Ashwin in a long silk tunic, standing in front of the Taj Mahal. I saw myself standing next to him, on a smooth white bench with Ashwin's camera hanging from my neck. We slept together in a tight bundle on top of Ashwin's sheets, tangled in each other's arms, until the next morning when I woke up, and he was gone.

It was late. Light streamed in just as it had the morning before, only this time it was cold and gray. This time, dark clouds hovered above. I closed my eyes. I opened them again. Then I went into the bathroom and splashed warm water on my face.

Ashwin wasn't in the kitchen. He wasn't in the living room, either, and, after waiting a few moments, I began to worry, noticing his car keys on the kitchen countertop—next to Stephanie's cookbook. Then a door burst open and Ashwin came rushing into the room. He was carrying a box with him, a large box filled with personal items, photographs and greeting cards which he set near the stove.

"You have to leave," he said.

"What?"

"Get your things."

I watched him disappear into a closet and come back with a broom. Outside, the boat was tied to the dock and covered in a thick black tarp, as if it had never been used.

"I don't understand," I said.

"Get out," he said, firmly.

Then he ran upstairs.

"What's going on, Ashwin?" I said, following him. "Why are you being this way?"

He ignored me, dragging a suitcase into the room, ripping it open, rummaging inside. He began removing plastic bags full of clothing—women's clothing—and hanging them in a closet nearby. Then he went into the dressers and took out condoms and lubricant and a pair of fuzzy handcuffs I had never seen before, that we had never used. He placed them in a bag.

"Whose are those?" I said, sounding shrill.

He was silent, checking the surrounding area, finding a place to conceal the bag. Then he turned to look at me.

"Whose, Ashwin?"

He said nothing.

"Is it your wife?" I said, shouting. "Is it Uma?"

He told me to get my things together and leave at once. I did as I was told, pulling a T-shirt over my head, throwing my underwear into my duffel bag, running downstairs to the front door—where I saw a huge car parked in the driveway, a white Lexus with chrome wheels.

"Oh, fuck," Ashwin said, coming up behind me. "Goddamn it."

A young couple got out of the car, an Indian couple with a small child. They were unloading their suitcases. They approached the front door. Ashwin pulled me aside. He was sweating.

"Listen," he said. "Just tell them you are my friend. Tell them you stopped by. Tell them you work with me"—he paused, panicked—"at the grocery store."

My heart dropped.

"But you're a dentist," I said.

He shook his head.

One evening, in high school, my father came home from a parent-teacher conference and asked me about a boy named Dylan Shaw. I didn't think he remembered. I didn't think he recalled that winter morning on Dylan's front doorstep, shaking his hand—he had made a lot of house calls in those days—but then he told me about the meeting my teacher had called, to discuss what had happened, and now he knew everything: the names, mostly, but also the violence. The time my shirt was ripped open and cold water was poured over my head. The time I was thrown into a Dumpster behind our school. The time Dylan and his friends chased me into a wooded area and took turns urinating on my face. I could see the terror in his eyes. He said they were bullies—they were afraid. They didn't matter. But he was wrong: *I* was the one who was afraid.

Everything mattered.

I drove home that morning and replayed the scene at the lake house, hoping for it to change. I went to the market, the mall, picking things at random, not caring what they cost. I drove to the restaurant where Ashwin had taken me on our first date. I reached my apartment at dusk, carrying my duffel bag up the stairs. Stephanie was in the living room. She was smiling.

"Where have *you* been all weekend?" she said.

I didn't tell her the truth. I didn't tell her about Ashwin. I felt like a fool. I'd stood quietly by while Ashwin explained to Dr. and Mrs. Acharya that the house was in order, the backyard maintained, the mail stacked neatly in the den, the boat still covered in its tarp, per their instructions, unused. I watched Dr. Acharya hand him five crisp hundred-dollar bills. Then I watched him disappear into the kitchen. They didn't ask me who I was. They didn't say a word. Moments later, when Ashwin walked me to my car, he explained to me that Dr. Acharya was his cousin—he had sponsored his visa. They had asked Ashwin to housesit for them while they were away.

I asked him who he really was and he shook his head.

"No one you need to know."

I went into my bedroom and threw my bag on the floor, realizing that I was alone. I stared at my bed, where, not long before, Ashwin had ripped off my clothes. Just then there was a knock at the door. I turned around. It was Stephanie. She was holding a bowl of popcorn in her hands.

"Where's my cookbook?" she said.

I couldn't control it; I started to cry. I was only relieved that it hadn't happened sooner, that it hadn't happened in front of Dr. Acharya or his wife, that I hadn't made a scene, pulling at Ashwin's clothes, leaving them to wonder what was wrong. ♦

if you see me, don't say hi

Deepak was my older brother, six years to be exact, which made him sixteen when I was ten. He was dark, the color of the walnut furniture in my parents' bedroom. I was fair. And it was often a joke among our family and friends: how different we were. Like shadow and light, they said. Like milk and coal.

Though I was small for my age, Deepak was very tall, with strong muscles in his shoulders and arms. His armpits smelled sweaty, like the raw onions my mother piled on top of our potato *shaak*. He would pick me up from school in my father's Toyota, blasting rap music from the speakers: Tupac Shakur and the Notorious B.I.G. It was 1994, and he wore oversized T-shirts above his baggy jeans. His thick wavy hair was always tucked under a cap. He wore a twenty-two-karat gold chain around his neck. We would ride around the neighborhood for a while, Deepak reciting every lyric to the song "Juicy." "It was all a dream!" he would say, as trees flickered by.

He was my guard. If a child my age happened to be harassing me at school, Deepak would wait for him on the playground.

"You want me to kick your ass?" he would say, getting right up into the kid's face. "You want me to kick your fucking ass?"

The harassment would stop there, but only for a short while; after all, I was an easy target. At school they called me all sorts of names: Ali Baba, Aladdin, Apu. They asked me about my father's 7-Eleven.

"We don't own a 7-Eleven," I would tell them. "We own a motel."

My teachers were oblivious. Once, after an exam, my fifth-grade teacher asked me to say something to him in Farsi.

"I don't speak Farsi," I said. "I speak Gujarati."

He stared at me blankly. "But you're Persian."

"I'm Indian," I said.

"Like a tomahawk?" said Ryan Gillespie, a red-haired boy who'd once pulled my pants down in front of the entire class. "My dad says all Indians are lazy boozers."

Everyone laughed.

I was frightened each morning on my way to school. During the Pledge of Allegiance, I held my breath like I did when we drove by a cemetery, wary of the vague expressions on my classmates' faces. My teachers made us watch movies on slavery and segregation and then told us we were lucky to be living in the greatest nation in the world. It seemed implausible even then.

In school, I learned very quickly what it meant to be brown: it meant that white kids only talked to you if they needed something, black kids only talked to you if no other black kids were around, and the rest of us wouldn't talk at all. Not that it mattered. There were only three of us, anyway: a Persian named Farzad, a Mexican named Flora, and me.

Every now and then, a classmate would tap me on my shoulder

and ask me to say something to them in "Indian." I was tempted to say *"ben-chod,"* which, when translated, means "sister-fucker." I taught them *"namaste"* instead.

"Namaste," they would say, folding their hands in prayer.

I never said it back.

I was too busy trying to shrink myself. My parents would blast holy *bhajans* from our back porch on Sundays and I would crawl into my bedroom and shove a pillow over my head. According to my father, Indian people were the source of everything: music, mathematics, and dance. I remember watching TV with my parents once when a Britney Spears video came on. I was embarrassed to be in their presence, watching her swing her hips around, but my father was enthralled.

"Look at this," he said. "Indians dance with their hips and now even the whites are dancing with hips."

"The whites don't have hips," my mother said, laughing.

And I, remembering to record the video so that I could masturbate to it in my room, said nothing at all.

I wasn't like Deepak. He had a way with girls—of looking at them, talking to them—that I never possessed. During the holiday of Navratri, my family would join other families at a rec center or a high school gym, where we danced around in a circle, wearing bright-colored clothes, and offered prayers to the goddess Durga. Invariably the children got away, to play basketball on the courts outside, or listen to music in their parents' cars, or drink beer purchased by some older cousin or friend. Deepak would disappear, returning later with a lazy smile on his face, his shirt unbuttoned, his hair tousled or flat. Once, he waved his finger in the air.

"Smell this," he said.

"Why?"

"Just do it."

Afraid that it was a prank, that he had stuck his finger in dog shit or his own ass, I ran away. But later, when he explained to me what he had done, that he had fingered a girl named Deepika behind a Dumpster, and that she had moaned and writhed on his hand, I wished I hadn't.

By the time he was a junior in college, Deepak had screwed half the Indian girls in our town—we lived in Bloomington, Illinois, in a small community surrounded by cornfields and a mall. Meanwhile, I harbored unrequited crushes on white girls. Girls with light brown hair, sparkling blue eyes, and long tanned legs in the summertime, who played tennis and swam laps at the country club and, unlike my cousin Monali, didn't have to bleach their arm hair or wax their upper lips. They were girls who seemed to know their place in the world without ever questioning it, who tromped down the hallways with swinging ponytails and fragrant perfumes, and who teased the athletes with a flick of their smile. They were the kind of girls who would never look at me, not even once, not then at least. Not yet.

There was one other way in which Deepak and I were different: it was that he, unlike me, was an idiot. Halfway into his junior year at a marginally ranked college, Deepak flunked out. My parents were aghast. They treated it like a death in the family, which it was, in many ways: the death of a future, the death of an education, the death of their dreams of raising a doctor. I remember the gloomy day when Deepak returned to us with his suitcases full of unused textbooks and clothes, piling them into his room, locking his bedroom door. He remained there all night, and didn't come out until late the next evening, pulling up a seat at the table and refusing the *daar, baath, rotli,* and *shaak* my mother was offering, pouring a bowl of cereal instead. Over the next few days, he sat around the house watching music videos on MTV, staring into his computer screen, flipping through magazines. He started eating voraciously: whole packages of doughnuts and the chocolates my parents had brought back from a trip to London, fried chicken from KFC. He wore sweatpants and collegiate T-shirts he'd purchased from the campus bookstore during his first week at school. In the afternoons, I would come home from school and find him in the same position I'd seen him in when I left, which was with his legs splayed over the couch, his hands in his pants. He got fat—very fat. So fat I wondered how he even bathed. He started to smell like the homeless people who lingered outside our parents' Best Western motel, drinking dark liquor or Colt 45. Sometimes he and my father would get into screaming matches, and my mother and I would exchange nervous glances in front of the TV. Once, Deepak didn't come out of his room for three whole days. When he finally did, he was wearing a rumpled white dress shirt over a pair of faded black slacks.

"I'm going to get a job," he said, triumphantly.

"Where?" my father asked.

"At a car dealership. They're hiring over at Ford."

My father snorted. "What car dealership? What nonsense." He was eating fried puris and dipping them in yogurt. A piece of puri hung from his chin. "Car dealership," he said, shaking his head. "I am buying cars and you are selling them."

But he never sold a single car, because he didn't get the job, and after three weeks of frustration, after arguing late into the night, my parents came to a decision: Deepak would join them in the family business. It was up to me now, their one and only hope, to realize their dreams.

As it turned out, I was well on my way. By then I was a sophomore in high school, an honor student, and a member of the chess club. I had a photographic memory, which meant that I spent the vast majority of my time listening to Warren G albums instead of studying for exams. I still managed to pull straight As. While Deepak went to the motel each morning, to learn about franchising and how to hide small portions of money from the IRS, I went to school, buoyed by the prospect of talking to a girl. And there were many: Cindy and Lisa, Rebecca and Kate. But all of them paled in comparison to Alicia, with her tanned legs, her pendulous breasts. She wore tight shorts and denim tops that practically burst at the seams. She had bright yellow hair that she groomed with a comb. Sometimes I would count the shades of gold in her hair. Once, she caught me staring at her when she turned around to pass back an exam.

"What?" she said, sharply.

I gawked at her. It was like the final moments before hitting a car. You know it's about to happen, you know there's nothing you can do about it, and yet you try, pointlessly, to avoid it.

"Nothing," I said. And then, just as she was about to turn back around, "I like your hair."

"What?"

"Your hair. It smells fresh. There's this Chinese girl who sits in front of me in Trigonometry, and her hair smells like fried food. But yours is clean. I like it."

I thought she would smile at me, the way she had smiled at other guys who paid her court, but she looked at me like I'd just soiled myself. Her nostrils flared as she turned around and twisted the bright silk slash of her hair into a knot, then inched forward in her seat. I told Deepak about this later, in my bedroom, after my parents had gone to sleep.

"You idiot."

He was drinking a beer, one of the many pony-necked bottles he'd taken from a crate in our garage, hiding it under his sweatshirt (even though he was twenty-one). He'd offered me a sip, and, when I'd refused, he'd said I shouldn't be such a pussy all the time.

"These white girls don't even see you," he said, taking a swig of his beer and stretching his legs over my bed. I was on the floor, studying the back pages of a Nas CD insert, memorizing the lyrics so that I could rap them out loud in the shower.

"All they see is what they can get from you."

"What do you mean?"

"Don't you study history?"

I shrugged.

I studied the variations of Alicia's skin tone, how it was mottled and red after gym class, and how it shifted from alabaster to bronze in the summertime. I studied the way her breasts rippled like Jell-O every time she came rushing into the room. I studied, still, the way she mispronounced certain words in Spanish class, never bothering to correct herself—never needing to. I studied the way she glided up and down the stairs with such ease you would have thought the whole school was built in her honor, a monument to her beauty, which, if it were up to me, would have probably been the case.

Deepak finished his beer, belched loudly, and tossed the bottle into my backpack.

"Get rid of it for me."

Then he got up and headed for the door.

"Where are you going?" I asked.

"Out."

"With who?"

"Friends."

I laughed. "You don't have friends."

It was true: the friends who'd once idolized Deepak, who sat around listening to whatever sordid exploits he'd gotten himself into, were all gone. They were in college now, studying to become doctors or pharmacists or dentists. Deepak spent his Friday nights in front of the television, playing video games.

"I have new friends," he said, smiling. And he walked out of the room.

The new friend was sitting on our couch one afternoon when I came home from school, eating popcorn and jiggling her legs up and down. She wore leggings and a pink sweater that hung precariously over one shoulder, revealing the brown slope of her skin.

"Hi there," she said, flashing a set of cherry-red nails.

Her dark hair was highlighted—orange strands over black ones—and her eyes were winged with mascara. She watched me as I dropped my backpack on the floor.

"I'm Deepika," she said. "You must be Deep's brother."

I remembered the night Deepak had walked up to me in the parking lot, raising his finger to my nose. I shook the image from my mind. She told me that Deepak was in the shower; they had gone swimming at my parents' motel after work.

"You work at the motel?" I asked.

She nodded her head. "Just until grad school. I'm studying epidemiology."

"Are you dating my brother?"

She paused, a subtle smile playing across her lips. "Why do you ask?"

"No reason," I said, sitting down beside her. "But if you were dating him, if you two got married, it would be weird."

"Why?"

"Because of your names: Deepak and Deepika. It sounds ridiculous."

She laughed out loud, showing all of her teeth. I didn't think it was that funny, but she dropped her bag of popcorn on the floor and held on to her gut, as if she were in pain. Then she grew still. "I don't know if we're dating," she said, quietly, and I knew, by the way she looked at me, by the way she looked at my brother each day after that, that she hoped they were.

Soon, I was prepping for college, graduating from high school. There was a weird energy in the air. Suddenly, the people who had spent four years tormenting me, calling me names, weren't so bad after all. It was like being trapped on an airplane with a bunch of people who were tired and miserable, and all of a sudden you were landing and everyone was in love. I would see classmates who previously ignored me take a sudden interest in my life. I saw Alicia once at the movie theater and she gave me a hug—she was going to community college that fall; she wanted to be a nurse. The day I left for school, Deepak helped me pack all of my things in milk crates and cardboard boxes and carry them out to my father's van. He slipped a bottle of vodka into my suitcase. He told me not to become an asshole at college. He said that he would visit me sometime, that we would get drunk on campus and that he would buy all my roommates and girlfriends a round of beer. But he never did.

When I came back for Thanksgiving, he was depressed again. My parents had purchased another motel, and Deepak was driving there three times a week to manage it. This time he'd lost weight. His face was slimmer. His waist had thinned out. He said very little at the dinner table before slipping out to a bar. The next morning, my mother sat down with me in the living room, frowning.

"It's that girl," she said.

"Which girl?"

But I remembered her name. "Deepika?"

She nodded her head. Deepak and my father were at work. My mother was in her dressing gown. We were quiet for a while. Then she told me, very discreetly, that two weeks earlier, Deepak had proposed to Deepika in the honeymoon suite at the motel, and that she had refused. I couldn't help myself. I laughed.

"What's your problem?" my mother said, sharply. "Why are you laughing?"

But I couldn't control it. It rose from my gut, bubbling over my lips. I dropped the remote control and hunched over the living room sofa, laughing and laughing, until tears streamed from my eyes.

"Be sharam," my mother exclaimed, throwing up her hands. "To laugh at your brother this way."

But later, in my bedroom, it was Deepak who laughed. We were drinking a beer—I'd developed a taste for it by then, along with Bailey's Irish Cream—when he shook his head.

"Don't listen to Mom," he said, pushing one of my baseball caps over his head. "She doesn't know what the fuck she's talking about."

I didn't know whom to believe, but after a few days it didn't seem to matter. As soon as I had arrived it was time to leave again, and I was packing suitcases with the sweaters I'd left behind, thick thermals and jeans, tall boots for the blustery treks to class. I kissed my tearful mother and shook my father's hand, and dodged Deepak's swift punch to my left shoulder. He could still overpower me—I had stopped growing, and, at five foot eight, I was far shorter than he.

This didn't seem to matter at school, where I noticed a budding interest from girls, Indian girls mostly, whom I mostly ignored. I continued to harbor crushes on white girls, only now they weren't so unattainable. At parties, I would touch their breasts or their ass as we navigated a crowd, filling their cups with rum punch, watching their lips turn purple or red. Sometimes I would go home with one of them, fumbling with the zipper of my jeans. I grew bolder, asking for one phone number and then another, taking them out for coffee, sometimes not calling at all. Once, a girl named Aubrey fell in love with me, showing up at my dorm room at 3 A.M., screaming and crying until the RA had to escort her home. I developed a thick skin, not minding when girls started calling me names, only this time it wasn't "Aladdin" or "Ali Baba" or "Apu"; it was "asshole"; it was "prick"; it was "motherfucker." Instead of asking me where I was from, they asked me how I could be so heartless and cruel. I realized that we weren't so different after all, the girls and I—that, when it came to love, everyone was from a foreign place.

Deepak certainly was. Shortly before spring break, he drove six hours to the University of Michigan and proposed to Deepika right outside her apartment. To everyone's surprise, and her parents' disgust and dismay, she said yes. My parents were thrilled; they threw a big party for Deepak and Deepika over spring break, inviting 150 people, renting long tables and chairs, setting up a tent and catering food from the local Indian restaurant, Mughal King. My father went to Sam's Club and bought ten bottles of Black Label scotch and thirty bottles of white wine. On a bright Saturday afternoon, Deepak and I unfolded chairs and carried bags of ice over our shoulders, dropping spoons into large vats of food: chicken tikka masala, two types of dal, potatoes and eggplant swimming in saffron-tinted oil.

I drank a beer in my bedroom. Deepak joined me. We glanced outside to watch the stream of my parents' friends in their saris the colors of tropical fruit candy. Deepak pulled back the curtain, frowning.

"It's like a circus down there."

I laughed.

"This will be you someday," he said. He chugged his beer and opened another one. I could tell, by his eyes, that he had been drinking somewhere before. He wore dress slacks and a collared white shirt, and he was examining himself in the mirror when he turned around and smiled. "Do you have a girlfriend?"

It was the first time he had expressed an interest in my life. Usually, when I talked about school, Deepak would nod along vacantly—as if he were listening to one of the many stories my parents had told about their childhoods in India, with the vague expression of someone who had never lived there before. But this time he was rapt.

"No," I said, shyly. Though this was a lie. I did have a girlfriend. Her name was Kara, and she had called three times that afternoon—in spite of my instructions not to.

"Why can't I come?" she'd asked. When I'd told her why, when I had explained to her the glaring differences between her world and mine, she had cried and cried until she couldn't breathe anymore, saying it didn't matter, that we were all just people in the end.

Two hours later, Deepak was drunk. I could tell by the way he was dancing. The DJ was playing Panjabi MC, and Deepak was waving his arms around like a rapper. I was talking to a girl I'd had tennis lessons with—Rachana Desai—who was a first-year at Yale. She wore a crushed silk sari. She talked about the Whiffenpoofs. She kept adjusting the straps of her bra. At one point I imagined myself kissing her, taking her up to my room. I imagined what she looked like between her legs, how dark or soft or wet. By then I'd had sex with three different girls—all of them white. All of them had rosy nipples and porcelain skin. All of them stripped off their clothes with a confidence I had never seen before in a girl. I was thinking about this when my cell phone bleated and I saw Kara's name in the window. I excused myself, winding my way through the crowd of uncles and aunties and friends, sneaking a beer from the bar, until I was alone in the house. I went upstairs, where I would be away from prying eyes, and opened the bathroom door.

"Oh, shit," I said, turning my head. "Sorry."

It was Deepika. She was standing in front of the mirror, adjusting the straps of her blouse. Her hair was spun up in a jeweled mound on top of her head. She looked beautiful. Normally she wore leggings and sweatshirts and gym shoes and socks, but here, in her colorful *lengha,* with a bindi between her brows, she looked regal. I had no idea she was crying. I didn't realize it until she turned her head.

"What's wrong?" I said.

"Nothing," she replied.

"I can leave," I said, backing away, ignoring Kara's missed calls. "I'll give you your space. I was just trying to get away."

"No, stay," she said. She took a tissue from the counter and dabbed the skin under her eyes. Then she laughed. "I feel like a cliché."

"The crying bride?"

"Bride-to-be," she said. "I was thinking about something you said to me a while back."

"Something *I* said?"

She nodded. "About Deepak and I, how if we ever got married it would be weird: our names. Deepak and Deepika."

I was surprised that she even remembered it; it had already been two years.

"I guess it is kind of weird," she said, staring at her reflection in the mirror. I remembered the way she had laughed in the living room when I had told her, dropping her bag of popcorn onto the floor. I wanted to ask her if she was okay, if she needed to talk, if my brother had done something wrong, but by then I had learned enough to know that sometimes, when a woman cried, it was best to say nothing at all.

Two years later, Deepak and Deepika got married, in a ceremony that made their engagement look like a small tea party. Kara wasn't invited to that, either, and, three days later, after fighting all night in my room, we broke up. Sometimes I would remember that night of the party and wonder what Deepika had been crying about. A year after their wedding, when Deepak and I had what will forever be referred to as "the fight," the thing that tore us apart, the thing that made us disavow each other and promise to never speak to one another again, I realized I never would.

▲▼▲

It started with a girl. Her name was Marissa, and she went to my med school. She asked me for directions to the medical library and I asked her for her phone number. She wasn't like anyone I had dated before. By the time she was twenty-four, Marissa had been to twenty-four different countries, posting pictures on her blog. She had long dark hair the color of red wine. Her eyes were like sapphires, but she was not beautiful in any conventional way. That is to say, it wasn't her looks that drew me to her. It was her voice, the funny things she said, the way her eyes flashed wildly whenever I told her a story about my day. Over time, her beauty revealed itself to me like an undiscovered painting in an unknown wing.

We spent our weekends exploring the city of Chicago, where we went to school—going to restaurants and thrift shops and nightclubs and bars. She had an appetite for new experiences, suggesting foods I had never tried before, that neither Deepak nor my parents would ever deign to eat—Indonesian, Peruvian, Ethiopian. If we happened to go to an Indian restaurant, Marissa would skip past the chicken tikka masala and go straight for the lamb *karahi*. She ate with her fingers, explaining that her best friend in grade school, Sangeeta, was Indian, and that she had taught her this when they were twelve. I was in awe of her. Unlike other white women, who viewed my background as a barrier, Marissa was happy to accept me just as I was. At times she would ask me how to say something in Gujarati, and I was reminded of being a child, in school, teaching my classmates to say *"namaste"* with their hands.

I taught her *"ben-chod"* instead.

"That's awesome," she said, laughing, and later, when a waiter happened to be rude to us at a French restaurant, Marissa got up from the table and said it: *"Arre ben-chod!"*

I knew, then, that I was in love.

I also knew I couldn't keep her from my family. By then, my mother had begun to suggest girls for me, some daughter of a friend who worked in an office or a bank—or, like me, was in med school. "Why have one doctor in the family when you can have two?" she'd say.

It went better than I thought it would; as it turned out, my parents had grown accustomed to the idea of mixed marriages. They brought up the friends whose sons and daughters had also married "whites," who had Hindu-Christian weddings and light-skinned children, and who assigned these children Indo-American names, names like Dillon, which, in Hindi, would have been spelled Dhilan. They had heard that white people loved Indian culture, anyway, and that it wasn't such a big deal after all. They were more than accepting; they were thrilled. I would have been, too, had I been announcing our engagement, but I wasn't. We'd only been dating for a year.

"Bring her home," my mother said, standing in the kitchen, frying a batch of samosas, making double of everything and wrapping it twice. "We want to meet her."

On a cold autumn morning, Marissa and I boarded an Amtrak from Chicago to Bloomington, where my father was waiting for us with his van. He helped load our luggage into the trunk, avoiding eye contact with Marissa as he opened the door for her, behaving more like a driver than a dad. I was instantly annoyed. I was annoyed, further, by the abundance of food on the dining room table. I had told my mother a sandwich would do—it was Thanksgiving weekend, and there was no need to overeat. But of course she didn't listen. She was solicitous, shuttling back and forth between the kitchen and dining room table, piling puris onto our plates, not bothering to ask if we were hungry. She pronounced Marissa's name "Mareesa," and she was overly chatty, telling her mundane facts about our town: about the groceries that were on sale, the two-for-one sweaters at Kohl's. Marissa's parents were both professors at Northwestern, and the one time we had gone to their house, we didn't talk at all, listening to Buddha Bar and drinking red wine.

"Your family is great," she said later, in the bedroom, when we were unpacking our bags. I wondered what she would think of Deepak. She hadn't met him yet. He was at the motel, manning the front desk. I asked my mother where Deepika was and she rolled her eyes.

"She has gone to her cousin's house in Michigan."

"Why?"

"I don't know."

"Why didn't Deepak go?"

She was silent. After a while she folded up the rest of the laundry and walked out in a huff. "I don't know," she said, traipsing up the stairs. "I don't know anything anymore. Nobody tells *me* anything in this house!" And she slammed her door.

That evening, Deepak walked into the living room and punched me on my arm.

"Where is this *gori* girl you're hiding?" he said.

"Her name's Marissa," I said. "And she's in the shower."

He stared at me blankly.

"I'm just kidding, man."

But at dinner, Deepak was quiet, staring down at his plate, responding to Marissa's questions with one-word answers. I was uncomfortably aware of how he towered over us at the table, his long arms folded across his chest. My parents asked Marissa about her house in Evanston, her friends at school, gazing up at her in wonder, absorbing each fact, but not Deepak. When Marissa asked Deepak how he enjoyed working at the motel, if he had any interesting stories to share, he snorted.

"It's a job," he said. "Not everyone can be as lucky as my brother."

"It's not luck," I said. "It's hard work."

No one said a word.

After dinner, I decided to take Marissa on a drive, maybe go for a beer. I asked Deepak if he wanted to join us, but he refused, saying he had work to do. Then, just as we were sliding on our coats, he changed his mind.

"Wait," he said. "I'll come."

He was chatty in our father's car, telling me which way to turn, asking Marissa questions, including her in his jokes. He even complimented her, saying it was nice of her to take time away from her family to spend Thanksgiving with us. I was surprised. I'd never heard Deepak compliment anyone in my life. He was a different person, eagerly suggesting we go to a new bar that had opened up on campus, encouraging Marissa to order whatever she wanted on the menu. When the waitress came by he looked up at her and smiled.

"Is Lauren working tonight?"

I stared at him.

The waitress scanned the room before pointing toward the bar. "She's over there," she said. "In the red top."

My eyes followed Deepak's to a young woman dressed in a red top and skinny jeans. Her stiff hair was frosted, her makeup shiny under the lights. Deepak waved to her and smiled.

"I'll be back," he said.

But he didn't come back, not until it was time to leave. By then, Marissa and I had had our fair share of beers.

"Is that a friend of yours?" I said, as we stepped into the chilly parking lot and approached our father's car. He didn't respond.

He drove home in silence. All night he remained in his bedroom, whispering over the phone.

The next morning, Marissa and I woke up early to prepare the turkey and stuffing and sweet potato pie, but Deepak stayed in his room. He didn't come out until the bird had been carved, explaining that he would have to go to the motel: one of the desk clerks had called in sick; it being Thanksgiving and all, he would have to fill in. No one said a word. My mother stared down at her plate. My father pretended not to have noticed. It was I who went after Deepak, following him into the driveway and grabbing him by his arm.

"Hey," I said. "What's going on?"

He looked impatient. It was then that I realized how much time we'd spent apart, how little we spoke. I couldn't remember the last time we had listened to an album together in my room. "Where are you really going?" I said.

He was silent.

"Where, Deepak?"

He turned his head.

"Are you going to see that girl—the one from the bar? Are you having an affair?"

He laughed. "An affair," he said, mockingly. "Only white people have *affairs*. Jesus, man, you already sound like one of them."

"One of whom?"

He didn't say anything.

"Why is Deepika at her family's house?" I said. "Why didn't you go with her?"

"Why are you involving yourself?"

"Because she's my sister-in-law."

He walked away. I caught a flash of Deepika crying in the bathroom. I followed him onto the road.

"You can't treat her this way," I said, shouting now. "You can't do that to people!"

He ignored me.

"You need to think about someone else for a change, Deepak. You need to think about Mom and Dad."

He paused to contemplate the rows of identical brick houses ahead of us, the metallic sky above. Then he shook his head.

"You know," he said, softly. "I like Marissa—I do. But to be honest, I'm a little surprised." He was staring at me now, scratching his head. "I figured that, if one of us ever brought home a white girl—if we ever did that to *Mom and Dad*—she would at least be beautiful."

I don't remember what happened next, only that we were struggling on the ground, shouting. Deepak was surprisingly weak for his size, capitulating to me easily. A neighbor came out of her house and started yelling, "Stop it. Stop it. It's Thanksgiving!" but we didn't listen. I said things that afternoon that I had never said before in my life, that I would spend a lifetime regretting, wishing I could revise: that my brother was a failure—a loser—and that, if it weren't for our family, he would probably be dead. I saw the fight drain from his eyes. I saw his fingers loosen their grip. I saw what was once anger fueled by love turn to indifference fueled by hate. I watched him stand up and brush himself off, heading toward his car, turning around to address me one last time. There were tears in his eyes.

"You're done," he said. "I mean it. Don't talk to me. Don't even look at me. If you see me on the street, don't say hi."

I didn't try to stop him as he slammed the door shut and drove away. I went for a walk. Later, when I came back into the house, my mother shot up from the dining room table and asked what was wrong. But I shook my head. It was then that I realized tears were rolling down my face, collecting at my chin. But I hadn't felt a thing. It was windy outside, I explained to everyone in the room, and something must have got caught in my eyes.

Six weeks later, after New Year's Eve, Marissa and I broke up. I never told her about what happened between Deepak and me in the driveway. I didn't tell anyone. Not even my own parents. The day after Thanksgiving, I made up an excuse about an exam I had to study for, forcing Marissa to play along. For weeks I was impenetrable, remaining silent for hours, avoiding Marissa's exhortations to open up. The more she tried to probe me, the more I pushed her away. I could have told her what Deepak had said; it wouldn't have been a big deal. Probably she would have laughed even, thrown her head back and made some witty remark. She wouldn't have hated him the way I did—that's for sure. Sometimes I think it was this fact alone that made me pull away from her: that she could so easily forgive someone. That I still could not.

Over the years, I dated girls at a distance, diving into my work, graduating from medical school and entering a rigorous orthopedic surgery program out of state. I used this as an excuse to avoid going home. For a while, my parents were oblivious, asking only if I had talked to Deepak recently, if we were in touch, reminding me of his birthday, apprising me of some minor incident—a fender bender, an illness, a problem at the motel—that afflicted his life. But after a while my mother grew suspicious, pressing me for details and, when I made something up, catching me in my lies. She asked me why we hadn't spoken, why he never mentioned me at home, why I never invited him to visit me once in a while. I had no answer. I assumed he and Deepika were fine, because one day I received an email from her inviting me home. It was my parents' anniversary. She was hosting a party. She signed the email, "Love, Deepika Bhabhi." I packed a small suitcase and booked the next flight.

There were thirty people in my parents' backyard when I arrived, drinking and laughing and eating. I saw Deepak in passing, but he didn't look at me. He was drunk, and Deepika was watching him from the kitchen window. She was pregnant. My mother had been waiting to tell me the news: that I was no longer just a brother; I was going to be a *kaka* as well. I was surprised. I spent all night watching Deepika answer questions about the baby, sipping a glass of cider. She had gained some weight in her face and her arms, but she still looked beautiful, just as radiant as she had that night of her engagement party. In fact, she was glowing, pausing to allow someone to touch her belly, take her picture, refusing to sit down when my mother insisted she take a break. Later that evening, I joined her in the kitchen and listened to her complain about my brother while she rinsed dishes in the sink.

"He can drown in his drink," she said, sharply. "I should never have married him."

But I knew, by the flicker in her eyes, that it was only a joke. I helped her dry the dishes and stack them in a pile on the counter. I led her to the couch. She wore a blue silk dress. Her belly pushed through it like a drum; she rubbed it with her hand.

"Do you need anything?" I asked. "Juice? Seltzer? Water?"

She shook her head. I was about to go outside to talk to one of the uncles who had just arrived when she called out to me from behind.

"Have you heard what he wants to call the baby?"

I turned around, shaking my head.

"Deep," she said.

I laughed.

Later, when my mother called to tell me it was over—that the baby was dead—I cried: for Deepak, for Deepika, for all of us.

In three years, I said three words to my brother: "I'm very sorry." I said them the moment he came back from the hospital. I said them in a sympathy card. I said them in an email, too. I wanted him back. I was sorry for everything. I broke my silence, crying on the phone with him until I couldn't speak anymore, until my throat closed up and I could no longer swallow. But he didn't say a word. He made a "Hmm" noise which meant that he acknowledged my apology but had nothing further to say. Then he hung up the phone.

We spent the next few years acknowledging each other from a distance. I congratulated him in person when they finally had a baby girl, Shreya, who weighed six pounds two ounces. She had soft brown eyes and hair as thick as wool. She looked more like Deepika than Deepak—which, I said jokingly, was fortunate. But Deepak said nothing. Sometimes I would ask him a question about work or his health and he would stare at me like I was an interloper. Once, we were in the kitchen reaching for the same beer when our hands locked. It was the first time we had touched each other since that night in the driveway. It was also the first time he had spoken more than two words to me.

"I was going to drink that," he said.

"So was I." I looked in the fridge. "It's the last one—split it?"

"No." He let go of my hand. "You have it."

I was flattered, buoyed by his generosity, but later, when he didn't talk to me for three days, I realized what he'd meant: that he would rather go without a beer than split one with me.

I moved to Los Angeles and drowned out the noise: my mother's complaints, her lengthy diatribes, the articles she would send me about the unexpected tragedies of life. Sometimes I would YouTube old music videos Deepak and I used to watch when we were young, remembering all the times I rode around with him in the car. Once, a girl I was dating paused in front of the mantel above my fireplace, pointing to a picture of Deepak and me in India—in matching black T-shirts, our hair slicked into spikes—asking me who he was.

"My brother," I said, and I was surprised by how quickly it rolled off my tongue, how easily he came to mind, as if I had been waiting for the right moment to mention him. As if I had been hoping she would ask me this all along.

Years ticked by like the hands of a faulty watch—quick, then slow—and finally, in the fall of 2015, forty years after my parents had first landed in America, thirty-three years after I was born, ten years after Deepak and I had stopped talking, my parents made an announcement: they were retiring. On the phone, my mother informed me that they would sell their motels to Deepak and spend six months in India, six months at home. The Indians in our hometown threw them a retirement party; I flew in from Los Angeles to attend it. Instead of having my father pick me up from O'Hare, I rented a car, preferring to drive past the rows of never-ending corn, the advertisements for shopping centers, the all-you-can-eat buffets. I stopped at a convenience store near my house and picked up some beer and a bottle of champagne. The cashier stared at me pointedly.

"Are you Premal Patel?"

"Yes," I said.

She could have been anyone, any blond-haired, blue-eyed girl from my past, but then I stared at her name tag, the swell of her breasts, and suddenly, it was clear.

"Alicia?"

I remembered the way she had looked at me in class that morning when I'd told her I liked her hair. She looked older now, with swollen cheeks and a few lines etched into her skin. Still, I was nervous, remembering all the hours I'd spent obsessing over her. She asked me what I was doing in town and I told her. Then she asked me what I did for a living. I could have told her that, too. I could have told her I was a doctor, a surgeon, that I saved people's lives. I could have made her feel small and insignificant, the way I had felt all those years. But I didn't.

"I work in health care," I said, paying for my items and signing the receipt. "In California."

She smiled.

"Well, it was good seeing you," she said, watching me head out into the bright summer afternoon. "Take care."

My parents' house was exactly the same. It was late summer, and the days were getting shorter. I saw my mother's suitcases piled on top of one another near the landing upstairs. They would be flying to London in a few days, and then to Mumbai, and then to Gujarat, where they would stay in a rented flat. I dropped my bag off in my room and freshened up in the bathroom. Then I took out one of the beers I had purchased and felt its warmth stream down my throat. I thought about the last time Deepak and I had drunk a beer together in my room, the night of his engagement party.

Downstairs, I was too preoccupied with the uncles and aunties who had, over time, become like second parents to Deepak and me, to notice him in the backyard, playing with his kids—by then, they'd had another child named Hiral. I was still single, still childless, still the source of my parents' anxiety. Deepika was drinking wine with me in the kitchen, teasing me about prospective brides, when her expression suddenly changed.

"He talks about you," she said, gravely.

She looked pretty in a sleeveless peach dress, a string of pearls at her throat. Her hair was shorter now, no longer streaked with highlights. "He says things like, Premal used to say this, or Premal used to say that. He asks the kids what they want to be when they're older. He asks them if they want to be a doctor like their Premal Kaka."

I was on my third glass of wine by then, but the news shattered the thin membrane of my buzz. "And what do they say?" I asked.

She laughed, gazing out the window.

"They say they want to be a businessman like their daddy."

I followed her gaze to the grassy knoll where Deepak was running around with a rubber ball, stopping frequently to bounce it over his children's heads. There was a plastic swing set that looked brand new, a tire that hung from a tree. The sun was going to set soon, casting a pinkish hue across the sky. By this time, most of the guests had left, leaving behind paper plates smeared with red chili sauce and half-eaten samosas. My parents had gone for a walk. We were alone in the house. I poured her another glass of wine.

"Oh, god. I think that's my third."

"Who's counting?" I said.

She laughed again, and I was reminded of the time in our living room when I had joked with Deepika about her name, and later, in the bathroom, when I'd seen her cry. She told me she didn't really understand what went on between my brother and me, why we drifted apart, but it didn't matter, anyway, because she was glad I was there.

"I miss you," she said. "I miss your sense of humor. We could use more of it around here."

"I miss being here, too," I said. I poured myself another glass of wine and felt the membrane envelop me again, loosening my tongue, so I asked her.

I asked her what I had been meaning to ask her all these years.

"Do you remember that night of your engagement party?" I said. "Do you remember running into me in the bathroom?"

She was silent.

"You were crying," I said.

She nodded her head. "I remember it."

"Why?"

"Why what?"

"Why were you crying?"

Her eyes clouded. I offered her another glass of wine but she shook her head, moving her glass away. Then she changed her mind, pushing it toward me. I emptied the bottle. She took a sip from it and shrugged.

"I don't know," she said. "I was practically a kid then."

"And?"

"And I didn't want to marry your brother," she said, firmly.

"Oh."

"Of course I love him now. We have a life together. It's all worked out for the best; it always does." She examined her glass before taking another sip. "Anyway, it was a long time ago."

I nodded, satisfied with her answer. Then I shook my head.

"But why?"

"Why what?"

"Why did you marry him? What made you change your mind? Your parents didn't even want you to marry my brother. Everyone knew that."

She laughed.

Then she told me that, just before I had walked in on her in the bathroom, she had been planning to leave. She'd told a friend to drive down from Michigan. They had it all planned out. She couldn't bear the thought of confronting Deepak about it, and my parents had spent all that money on the party, so she was going to run away, disappear, change her phone number, her email address. She spoke rapidly, pausing to laugh at something or to catch her breath, taking a sip of her wine. And then it happened: I watched her lips moving and felt the strange compulsion to kiss them. To feel them. To know, once and for all, what my brother had known all those years.

"But then you stopped me," she said. "I don't know what it was. There was something about the way you were looking at me—this kindness, this innocence—and I thought to myself: there must be some of that in Deepak, too." She smiled. "And there was."

I asked her if Deepak knew about it. She shook her head.

"Are you kidding me? He would flip."

We were silent for a while, drinking the rest of our wine, staring at the pink and purple clouds outside our window, when I reached for her hand. She pulled it away. I reached for it again. I pulled her close to me, forcing myself against her, until finally, she gave in. Instead of kissing her, I wrapped my arms around her and felt the give of her shoulders, the slack of her spine, the warm rush of her tears, dampening my shirt. We'd both had enough wine by then, and I helped her rinse the glasses and dispose of the bottle, too. Then I followed her outside, where Deepak was standing on the patio with a beer in his hand, watching the kids from a distance.

His hair was beginning to gray now, and his midsection had widened, but he still retained the impressive fact of his height, the same span of his shoulders, the same girth of his arms, and I still admired these things from afar, crossing the patio to join him, waiting, as usual, for the Deepak I once knew to return.

Eight months later, he did, after our father died unexpectedly in the middle of the night—he'd had a heart attack. My mother was inconsolable. It was Deepak who came to pick me up from the airport. We didn't talk much on the car ride home, preferring to listen to music on the radio instead, but later, in the kitchen, he told me the news.

"Deepika is leaving."

I was stunned. He said it was over—they had tried to make it work, but somehow, in the end, the trying wasn't enough. I asked him if the divorce was his idea, if it was something that he wanted, and I knew, by the soft, sad look in his eyes, that it was not. So I held him for a while, sitting on our kitchen floor, crying: for Deepika, for my father, for the things we never knew. ♦

the taj mahal

It was Mallory who introduced us in the first place: at the shopping mall, then her party.

It was winter; I was visiting from L.A.

"L.A.," Mallory said. "Wow."

There was nothing *wow* about it. The hospital had put me on leave—something about "indecent behavior." As far as I was concerned, I was the best OB/GYN they ever had.

"You've unraveled," Dr. Barnes said. "The rest of the staff feels uncomfortable around you."

"On what grounds?"

"On the grounds that you exposed yourself to Dr. Rosenberg."

"I did no such thing."

"You offered him sex."

"That's preposterous," I said, glaring. "That's the dumbest thing I ever heard."

Then I took off my blouse.

It wasn't always this way; in high school, Mallory was the adventurous one. Mallory was the one who got drunk off rum punch and strawberry Boone's. Mallory was the one with the tattoo; now she wore rust-colored sweaters and khaki-colored slacks, looking, at thirty-two, like the type of woman we swore we'd never be. We ran into each other at Target, on a Saturday afternoon. Mallory pushed a shopping cart.

"Sabrina? Is that you?"

After high school, I had become glamorous while everyone else in my class had faded out of their glamour. Mallory included. She had a thick waist, loose skin; her blond hair had faded to brown. Meanwhile I was bronzed like honey, my hair the color of a cocoa bean. I wore extravagant clothes. The night of Mallory's party, I wore a raspberry cocktail dress from Neiman Marcus.

But it was meant to be a casual party.

I told her there was no such thing.

The party was typical: cheese boards next to a platter full of crackers and grapes. Mallory had strung up Christmas lights—colored ones, not gold. All night long she chased me around the house carrying store-bought appetizers and boxed red wine. She introduced me to her friends. They were the usual sort: women who wore Christmas cardigans over stonewashed jeans. Their makeup was of the drugstore variety. Probably they were schoolteachers or nurses and probably they were afraid of me because I was a surgeon. A specialist. A god.

Sabrina lives in L.A. Can you imagine?

They couldn't imagine. They couldn't imagine that a week ago I had gone to a dive bar and popped a Klonopin into my mouth—then gone home with the DJ. His name was Yousif, and the next morning, four hundred dollars were missing from my purse. They would never understand me, these women, so I smiled at them, and nodded my head, and answered their questions about the traffic in L.A., and then, when I couldn't stand it any longer, I opened my bag and popped another Klonopin into my mouth. Then I started drinking. When I returned, Mallory had opened a bottle of champagne. *Happy holidays, everyone!* I imagined spilling it on her floor. I wondered if she would get on her hands and knees to clean it up. I was thinking about this when Mallory's boyfriend walked into the room, opening a can of beer, and suddenly, just like that, I began to think of something else.

I had no boyfriends of my own: I'd hoped Dr. Rosenberg could be my boyfriend. One morning, we were sitting in the doctors' lounge when I showed him a book I had read on giving really good blow jobs. Dr. Rosenberg had laughed, but later, when I showed it to him again, he didn't seem so amused.

"We're in a meeting, Sabrina, and you're being very inappropriate."

Mallory's boyfriend would have laughed. Mallory's boyfriend worked for a tire shop called Geeks on Wheels. He had a finely trimmed beard. There was something intriguing about him. He wore an Illinois sweatshirt over jeans. He had a dab of Brie on his chin. He stood near the cheese plate and avoided conversation. I walked over to him and spilled my drink on his shoes.

"Oops."

"It's okay," he said. "They're not fancy like yours."

I laughed louder than necessary. "I'm Sabrina," I said.

"Mallory's friend, right?"

"Classmate. We went to high school together."

"Right. I'm Dave."

"Dave," I said. "The boyfriend."

"Dave-the-boyfriend."

"Well, Dave-the-boyfriend, I could really use a smoke right now. Know where I can make this happen?"

He pointed toward the kitchen.

"Back porch. You'll see a life-size cutout of Santa Claus. You can't miss it."

"That's where I'll be."

I could sense him watching me as I made my way through the kitchen, onto the patio beyond. When I stepped outside, the giant Santa Claus was staring me in the face. The backyard was silver with moonlight and the branches were stripped bare. I heard the squeak of a door.

It was Dave-the-boyfriend. He was holding a beer. From an open window, I could hear someone suggesting a game of Taboo.

"It's supposed to snow tonight," he said.

"I like the snow."

"I guess you don't see much of it where you're from," Dave said.

"Mm."

We were silent a moment; then Dave sat next to me and stared at my cigarette.

"Want one?"

"I can't. Mallory wants me to quit."

"Mallory's not here."

He smiled.

"Aren't you some kind of doctor? Shouldn't you be condemning this?"

"I'm an OB/GYN," I replied. "Are you pregnant?"

"No."

"Then as far as I'm concerned you have nothing to worry about."

He took the cigarette from my hands. His nail beds were dirty.

I found this irresistible. He exhaled a plume of smoke; then he closed his eyes.

"God, I needed that."

"It's our little secret," I said, crossing my fingers.

We stayed like that for a while, Dave and I, until the cigarette was finished and the evening turned cold. Then he flicked the cigarette into the bushes and brushed off his jeans.

"I better get back inside. Don't stay out here too long."

I followed him inside, where Mallory was opening a bottle of champagne in the kitchen. She looked even larger than I had remembered. "My god!" she said, handing me a glass. "You're shivering!"

The thing about being an OB/GYN is that everyone wants to talk to you about their vagina: how to get pregnant, how not to get pregnant, how to get rid of embarrassing smells.

"Your vagina is like a self-cleaning oven," I said. "Stay away from harsh soaps."

The women flocked to me. Mallory linked hands with Dave and paraded him around the room.

"It's supposed to snow tonight," she told me.

"So I've been told."

"So what brings you in town? Are you visiting your parents?"

My parents were dead; they'd died in a car accident last year. Nobody knew. When the clinic put me on leave, the first thing I did was purchase a last-minute fare to Urbana, Illinois. Then I got drunk in my room. I planned on sticking around for a while, putting the house on the market. I did not plan on running into Mallory or Dave.

"I'm just home for the holidays," I said. "It being Christmas and all."

"I see," Mallory replied, going back into the kitchen.

Dave was staring at her, narrowing his eyes. I wondered if he was in love. Then I realized that nobody who loved somebody would smoke a cigarette behind her back.

So I opened my bag.

"Let's smoke another one."

Someone had decided to play Christmas carols on the hi-fi system, and there was a game of charades in the living room, so no one noticed when Dave and I slipped out through the back door. The night felt colder; Dave offered me his coat. His sleeves were rolled up and I could see the tattoo on his arm.

"I have a tattoo," I said.

"Oh, yeah?"

"Yeah. But you can't see it."

"Why not?"

"Because it's on my vagina."

He spit out his drink. We sat down in front of the life-size Santa Claus and Dave was looking at my legs. Suddenly I wasn't so cold anymore.

"I hate Christmas," I said.

"I've never heard that before."

"That's because you're dating Mallory."

"Which reminds me," Dave said. "Back there, inside, you said that you and Mallory were classmates."

"Right."

"I asked if you were friends."

I stared at him, narrowing my eyes.

"You're not just a mechanic, are you?"

"I dropped out of law school."

"Why?"

"Because I'm an idiot," Dave said, putting out his cigarette. "And because I thought I was in love."

He went inside to get more beers and we drank them one by one, crushing the cans. The music grew louder, and every few moments there was an undulating cheer. Dave was getting drunk. His eyes had glazed over. Meanwhile I was barely buzzed. On a normal night, I had a whole bottle of wine to myself. Sometimes I got so drunk that a piece of forgotten memory would return to me in the middle of the night. Once, I had woken up wearing someone else's brassiere. An idea suddenly sprang to mind. I grabbed Dave by the arm. "Let's get out of here. Let's go for a drive. No one will know."

"I don't know . . ."

"I've got ecstasy," I said, dropping my voice to a whisper. "And marijuana."

There was a loud crash from within the house. Mallory was screaming about the turkey. She ran around the kitchen and began calling Dave's name.

But it was too late.

I don't normally drink and drive, but when your parents die in a car accident, you begin to form your own rules. The world is fucked up as it is. What difference does a few drinks make? I pulled out of Mallory's driveway in my father's red Porsche. I felt the heat from Dave's skin. We stopped at a liquor store so Dave could buy more beer. While he was gone, I adjusted my makeup. I put on red lipstick because I had read once that red lips made men think of all the other places you were red. Then I powdered my nose. My dress, the tube of sequins that cost $850 at Neiman Marcus, had ridden up my thighs. I liked it this way. I felt a throbbing between my legs. I tried to remember the last time someone had touched me there—then I remembered it was only last week, with the DJ. When Dave returned he opened a can of beer and fastened his seat belt, kissing me on the mouth.

"Oh," I said, melting.

Dave's mouth tasted like menthol cigarettes; his lips were rough and dry. We kissed some more, until our hands were in places that were not so rough—not so dry.

"Fuck," he said, slapping the dashboard. "I shouldn't have done that. I'm sorry."

I thought about Mallory and her party and that stupid life-size Santa Claus.

I put my hand on Dave's thigh. "I'm not sorry."

My parents' house was like one of those houses on TV, where the father has an affair and the daughter runs away. It was tall and stately and pushed back from the road. The inside was full of polished white stone. We entered the foyer. I turned on the lights. Dave's eyes grew wide. I could see him more clearly now. He had broad shoulders, sculpted arms. I wondered what the rest of him was like.

We drank in the kitchen. Every few minutes, Dave would glance around the room and point out something he liked. I found this annoying; I wanted him to like *me.* I wanted him to ask about my job. Instead he put his drink down and shook his head.

"This is so weird."

"What is?"

"This. Us. Together."

"What's weird about it?"

He looked at me the way Dr. Rosenberg had looked at me, the

way everyone looked at me these days. Then he shrugged his shoulders.

"I guess you're right," he said, reaching over to pour himself a scotch. "Hey, how about showing me around?"

In high school, you knew you were rich when people wanted a tour of your house. No one ever walked into a duplex and said: "I *have* to see this." The kids in my grade, the ones who rode the bus to school, referred to my parents' house as the Taj Mahal. It looked nothing like it. But we were Indian, and the distinction between them and us was clear. My father was a urologist. My mother was a professor of physics. I explained this to Dave when he paused to glance at some artifact or painting. After their death, I'd gone home for the weekend and systematically removed every trace of them from the house: the portraits and clothing and expensive leather shoes. My mother's perfumes and saris were packed away in a box. Her wedding jewelry was melted down and sold. The albums in which I stood between them in pigtails sat at the bottom of a dustbin. It was my aunt who'd phoned me with the news. I was in residency, at a hospital in L.A. After hanging up the phone I'd vomited, then cried.

My childhood bedroom was plastered in pink; there were pictures of myself all over the walls.

"You look scared," Dave said.

"What?"

"These pictures." He pointed to one in particular. "You look nervous. Like you're afraid of something."

No one had ever told me that before. In high school, Mallory and I were queens. Every Sunday morning we met at each other's houses to organize our outfits for the rest of the week. Sometimes we would exchange blouses or tops; once, we stole a pair of culottes from the Buckle. It was Mallory's idea.

"Weren't we all afraid of something back then?"

Dave was silent, taking this in. He sat on my bed. After a few moments I joined him. We said nothing for a while, dangling our legs, until the silence was broken and the words tumbled out of my mouth: "I never liked Mallory, actually."

And then we were kissing again.

The first time I kissed a boy was in this very room. It was summer, and Mallory had invited someone over: a boy named Calvin Rhodes. His tongue made circles inside my mouth. He unbuttoned my pants. We were listening to Missy Elliott while it happened. I was only sixteen, but I had seen all of the films, had learned all of the moves. I used my imagination to fill in the gaps. When it was over, Mallory came running into the room. *Tell me everything,* she'd said.

And I did.

It occurred to me that Dave was the type of man my parents had forbidden me to marry. I wondered how it would work, marrying Dave. I wondered what my friends would say. They were mostly doctors or lawyers or people who invented things. They didn't know any mechanics. *He's just figuring things out,* I would tell them. *He was in law school, you know.*

It might be nice having a man around the house. He could fix things. There was that crack in the bathroom. There were the dogs, too. My neighbor kept Alsatians; they were always barking at me. I pictured Dave chasing the dogs away. I pictured us getting dogs of our own. Maybe Dave would wrestle with them and I would bake pies and then he would come into the house smelling like dog sweat.

He unsnapped my dress, letting it pool at my feet. He took off his shirt. It was nice in the way it was meant to be. Dave was competent, sweet, even. He took his time. Then my mind began to wander and I said something I probably shouldn't have.

"I don't know what happened . . ."

"What?"

"Mallory," I said, blinking. "She used to be thin—thinner than all of us. It was her thing: thinness. And now look at her."

It was the wrong thing to say. Dave was silent, wiping his brow. He pushed himself off me.

"I think we should go."

"What—why?"

"Because it's getting late."

"But we were only getting started."

"I think we've gone too far."

He fumbled with his jeans. He buttoned up his shirt. After a few moments he gave me a look I will never forget.

"Mallory has hypothyroidism," he said. "She's been having a tough time."

I should have told him I was sorry. I should have told him it was a mistake. Instead I told him the truth: that hypothyroidism was really no big deal. Dave gave me a look of such loathing that I felt the hairs on my neck stand on end.

"Mallory will be waiting."

"But you haven't even finished your drink."

"I've had enough."

"But we were having such a good time."

"She *needs* me," Dave said, crossing his arms.

And the room went red.

I picked up Dave's drink and examined it under the lights—then I poured it out on the floor.

"Well, isn't that nice?" I said, watching the stain spread. "What a wonderful boyfriend you are."

By the time we returned to the party it was in full swing. Dave put his hand on my arm.

"Maybe you shouldn't come inside."

I didn't argue; instead, I watched as Dave unbuckled his seat belt and slipped out of my car.

"I thought it was supposed to snow," I said, following him.

But he didn't answer me. He sprinted across Mallory's front lawn. When he didn't return, I walked around to the trunk of my car. Somewhere behind my father's golf clubs and tennis shoes was an emergency kit with a box full of tools. I pulled out a hammer. I slung it over my shoulder. I squeezed through the bushes and went around to Mallory's back porch. Beyond the windows, I could hear Christmas carols and the sound of Mallory's high-pitched voice piercing through the night. I saw her shadow through the curtains. She wouldn't ask Dave where I was. It wasn't her style. Before I knew it, I was standing on Mallory's back porch, looking up at that ridiculous life-size Santa Claus, its pink face grinning at me. It was probably the largest one around. It was like Mallory to do that, to steal the attention away from everyone else, the way she had stolen Calvin Rhodes right from under my nose. I raised the hammer over my head.

I swung at it but missed. I swung again, this time striking it between the eyes. I kept swinging, sometimes missing, sometimes breaking a limb, sometimes losing the hammer altogether, until there was nothing but a heap of red and white scraps piled up on the ground. Then I began to swing at everything else: empty flower pots, a yellow pinwheel, three decorative gnomes all lined up in a row. I did this until my hair was flat and my arms were sore and my red sequined dress had a tear running down its side. I started remembering things, too: the time I got a bad haircut and Mallory invited everyone over to see it, the time I lost my favorite earrings and Mallory showed up with them at the prom, the time Mr. Moncrieff made all of us watch *Indiana Jones and the Temple of Doom* and Mallory told the entire class that it was true: she had seen *my* parents eating monkey brains as well.

I saw her face in the window. She was looking right at me. After a few moments, she opened the door.

"You'll freeze to death out here."

I told her I was already dead. Mallory lit a cigarette and walked over to where I was standing, reaching for my hand.

"Don't tell Dave about this," she said. "I told him to quit." We were silent, gazing out across the yard. Then Mallory let go of my hand and started to cry.

"It's not fair."

She was drunk—she would never have mentioned it otherwise. She began sobbing into her hands. "I never knew," she said. "You never told me, but then someone mentioned the accident and now it's all I can think about. Oh, Sabrina. What happened?"

I tried to remember the last time I had seen my parents alive. It was last Thanksgiving, and my father had burned the turkey. Three days later, he drove into a guardrail.

I took the cigarette from Mallory's hands. I flung it into the bushes. I looked up and saw something moving over our heads.

"It's snowing," I said.

"It is?"

Mallory spun around, reaching for my hand again. The snow fell like diamonds, glistening in her hair. ♦

the other language

Sometimes, at night, I heard my parents complaining about me in the kitchen, arguing over which one of them had failed. I was not like their friends' kids, who won spelling bees and math competitions, spent their summers learning French. Though my father was a doctor, I had no aspirations of becoming one. I spent my evenings alone, in my bedroom, watching MTV. During commercial breaks I listened to my parents condemning me from below, wondering how I could be so unremarkable. They spoke in whispers, in Gujarati, but sometimes, when I had done something particularly shameful, they spoke in another language entirely: Swahili.

Though my parents were Indian, they had never lived in India—their parents had left India to help the British build the rail. My father was from Kenya, my mother from Uganda. Our house was filled with the evidence: wooden elephants and charcoal drawings of Maasai people holding spears. All throughout the basement were videos of African wildlife and photographs of my father standing in front of wildebeest. Sometimes I heard them whispering about how dangerous it was, how lucky they were to have left. I'd heard stories about servants revolting against their employers and stealing their gold. I'd heard about Faraji, my uncle's gatekeeper, who'd locked him in his bedroom while hoodlums looted his home. It was dangerous to be an East Indian in East Africa, they said. So I was surprised when my father came downstairs one evening and announced to everyone that he had closed his office for the month. Our tickets were booked. We were going to Kenya for three weeks in December and I would be missing school.

On a winter morning, I awoke to my alarm clock and stared outside at the large piles of bluish-white snow. What a difference it was, later, to see the spiky greenery outside Jomo Kenyatta airport. We had arranged to stay with Rajesh Kaka in a white mansion on Riverside Drive.

"Patel family—this way."

A large man ushered us through the crowd. I had never seen so many people: women in caftans, merchants selling beads, African tour guides holding up pictures of leopards and gazelles. We approached a white Jeep parked on a mound of thick red clay. Red dust colored our skin.

"*Jina langu ni* Jozi," he said. "Your driver for this evening."

Jozi gave us juice boxes and french fries and we ate them in the backseat of his car. My sister made a face. She was sixteen—less concerned with Africa and more concerned with her Mariah Carey CD. She complained about the insects, the heat, but mostly, the absence of her friends. I had no friends of my own, and thus complained of nothing.

The servants took our bags. I was on the first floor, in a wood-paneled apartment overlooking the pool. Outside my windows were banyan trees and clusters of palms. I explored the room for a while before taking a nap—we had been traveling for days, and I could still hear the aircraft's engine in my ears. It was nightfall when I awoke. Rajesh Kaka was serving my parents a drink on the lawn. Nirmila Aunty, his wife, sparkled at his side. "Do you know who I am?" she said, rushing over to me in a silk tunic, smothering me in her breasts.

I told her I did.

That night, we grilled fresh *mogo* with red chili and lime (that starchy snack my parents could never replicate in the States). Nirmila Aunty was solicitous, Rajesh Kaka, too. He would laugh that raucous laugh of his before ordering more food. He yelled at a houseboy for dropping a pan.

"Watch your things," he later told us. "These people are thieves."

My father was dozing. My mother was drunk. My sister was fiddling with her Discman. I decided to take a walk. I entered the kitchen and opened the fridge, staring at the contents: mason jars filled with red pickles, bottles of white wine. I heard someone call my name; it was a houseboy. He was smiling.

"Need something?"

He looked my age, with skin like chocolate, eyes like graphite, thick, kinky hair that glistened as if wet. His name was Kito. He wore white Nikes that looked brand new. I was surprised; most of the other boys wore sandals.

"I live just there," he said, pointing to a small crumbling compound Rajesh Kaka had pointed out that morning: the servants' quarters. I told Kito I wanted a cup of Milo. He opened the cupboard.

"I can do it," I said.

He ignored me, fetching a jug of milk, mixing the Milo with a spoon. I was embarrassed: he was my age and he was serving me. He placed the Milo next to a plate of Jaffa Cakes and coconut macaroons. When I was finished eating, he cleared my dishes in the sink.

"You like football?"

"Yes," I lied.

"Good. We can play tomorrow."

My heart leapt. I had never played sports before.

"Where are you from?"

"Chicago."

He smiled. "Michael Jordan."

It was a lie—I was from a small town two hours south of Chicago. I lied about something else, too. I lied about having a girlfriend. I don't know why. Maybe it was because he had built this image of me in his head—the prosperous American—and I didn't want to disappoint him. "I have a girlfriend, too," he said. "Her name is Aisha."

He reached inside his pocket to show me a picture. Before he could do so, Rajesh Kaka came storming into the room. *"Basi toka!"* he yelled. "Get out!" And Kito disappeared into the night.

The next morning, we ate breakfast by the pool: sausages and mangoes cut up into bright cubes. My sister complained about the sun.

"I'm getting black," she said, loud enough for the servants, most of whom were darker than she was, to hear.

We went shopping for textiles and jewelry and little handmade statues of elephants and giraffes. I asked my mother for a woven bracelet threaded with the colors of the Kenyan flag. She snatched it from my grasp. "What kind of boy wears bracelets?"

I missed my video games, my room. I missed my comic books. I was not used to this place of watchfulness, where it was impossible to be alone. At night, my parents and Rajesh Kaka drank Tusker Lager on the back lawn and gossiped about our family: the ones who were well, the ones who were ill, the ones who had run off and married a Muslim. They talked about my cousin Bijal, who'd scored a 1580 on his SAT. They talked about my sister's straight As. They talked about the neighborhood wunderkind who was a sophomore at MIT. They didn't talk about me. At home, I was an unfortunate consequence of parenthood, the kind of child you learned to tolerate—never accept. So I stayed indoors, listening to the orchestra of winged insects outside my bedroom door. I read the dog-eared copies of *X-Men* I had brought with me on the plane. I counted down the days before I would return home to America, to Illinois, to Urbana, and to the safety of my room.

Fortunately, we would be going to the bush next week—I was excited for that. I told Kito about it while we were dipping our feet in the pool.

"You like lions?" he said. "You'll see many, and wildebeest, too. Maybe if you are lucky you will see a leopard, but not likely. They hide."

I asked him about tigers and he laughed.

"No tigers in Africa."

I told him I was joking. I thought he would ask me to play soccer with him, but he took off his shirt. His body was lean and rippled, making me ashamed of my own. He dove into the pool. I went into my bedroom to change, fretting over the slight paunch I had developed, the feminine swell of my hips, but when I walked outside he was nowhere to be found.

It was like that for a while. He would find me throughout the day, poking me in the rib, asking me about the weather in Chicago, or if I had met anyone famous. He brought me treats from the kitchen. I'd see him sweeping the compound and he'd turn around and wave. Once, he threw a ball in my direction, a white cricket ball with a gash down its center. I was grateful for his company. I had never felt so comfortable in the presence of another boy. My own family did not offer me this comfort. At school, I kept to myself, my eyes lowered, my head bowed, as if in constant prayer. I was so afraid of saying or doing the wrong thing that I said and did nothing at all. But through Kito's eyes a new version of myself emerged. His interest in me, his questions about my world, gave me a sense of purpose I had never felt before. I began to anticipate the times I would see him, full of curiosity about my life, and lament the times I did not. It occurred to me, in those moments at least, that he was my only friend.

Our days developed a pattern. My father drank at the local pubs while my mother went shopping with Nirmila Aunty. My sister and I sat around reading Nancy Drew. She complained about the humidity, the heat, our parents, how aloof they seemed here, absorbed in Nairobi in a way that *we* could never be. I sat and listened to her before my mind would begin to wander, thinking of questions to ask Kito.

"How old are you?"

"Sixteen."

"How many siblings do you have?"

"Three."

"Where are your parents?"

"Gone."

I lowered my head.

"Sorry."

He frowned, mentioning a car accident when he was three; then he threw me the cricket ball. I couldn't imagine losing my parents—and yet I had wished for this very thing, had prayed for it once, after arguing with them all evening. That I could think such horrible things in front of Kito made me ashamed, an emotion I had only recently begun to understand.

We played catch. I was shaky at first, shielding my face. Kito laughed. He showed me the proper form. He taught me about wickets and runs. He guided me with his hands. He laughed at me when I made a mistake and applauded me when I did something right; sometimes, when I didn't listen, he would scold me in a deep tone. Fortunately there was no one else. I lived in fear those first few days that one of the other boys, Joseph or Jamal, or a girl even, Esha or Kesi, would join us in a game, that my weaknesses would be exposed. But it was just us. Long afternoons were spent running after the ball, throwing it in the air, drinking *madaf*—fresh coconut water from the market up the road—under one of the banyan trees overlooking Rajesh Kaka's pool. Sometimes he would show me things: a book or a game or a pair of headphones he had brought home from the store. In the evenings, Kito returned to the servants' compound and I was left to wonder about it: what the walls were like, what sort of things he had in his room. Once, he embraced me when I had successfully launched a cricket ball over his head and into the neighbor's backyard, his warm limbs damp against my skin.

By the end of the week I had made up my mind: I no longer wanted to go on safari. I knew what it would be like: my parents whispering in Swahili, my sister scowling at them from behind,

Rajesh Kaka barking out orders in the front seat. I asked my mother if I could stay home.

"Don't be ridiculous," she said. "It's one of the reasons we're here."

"But I'm sick," I cried.

She handed me some medicine. Her room was full of junk: silk garments, khaki shorts, an envelope, plump with money, stiff shillings she plucked to tip a driver or a maid. She caught me eyeing the envelope and pushed it aside. Then she rummaged through her purse. Finally she stood up and placed her hands on her hips.

"I can't find my gold watch," she said, staring at me. "Have you seen it?"

I shook my head. She panicked, opening drawers, flinging garments across the room, sifting through every piece of gold jewelry in her handbag. Eventually she threw up her hands. "All right," she said. "Go and ask your father."

The next morning, I stood on the verandah while the servants loaded up Rajesh Kaka's Jeep, my mother and father bickering over the luggage, my sister giving me murderous stares.

"He's faking it," she said.

Moments later, I was seeing them off, promising not to give anyone too much trouble. I would be under Nirmila Aunty's care. The Jeep rolled away in a cloud of red dust. I walked out onto the patio, where Kito was sunbathing on a strip of cement by the pool.

"You're here."

"I didn't feel like going," I said. "I was sick; I'm better now, though."

He nodded, light trembling over his face in shimmering gold swirls. He got up from his seat.

"Good," he said, toweling himself off. "Because I have something to show you."

He pulled out a flyer, flashing it in front of my face. It was for a cricket match. "I want you to be on my team."

"Are you sure?" My heart lurched. In school, I was picked last for team sports. I told Kito this and he laughed. He said the match would take place that evening, at a field near the city; he couldn't do it without me. I couldn't possibly refuse.

All day I was anxious. I paced the patio, wandered the halls, approached the servants' compound outside. It was different from Rajesh Kaka's house, a string of tiny dorms with geckos running up and down the walls. There was a large iron tap covered in thick green moss at the center of the courtyard. One of the houseboys was crouched in front of it, staring at me. I went back home. Hours later, I was reading my comic book in a hammock when I saw Kito stroll through the gates, carrying a sack of groceries in his arms.

"For your dinner."

I followed him into the kitchen, where I watched him unload meats wrapped in butcher paper, onions stripped of their skins, fresh green coconuts from the market down the road. He was wearing a long-sleeved blue shirt; when he reached up into one of the cabinets, the cuff slipped back to reveal a shiny gold watch.

I turned my head.

"You're dressed up," I said.

He opened the fridge, rummaging inside. I remembered my mother searching through every piece of gold jewelry in her handbag, throwing up her hands. I thought about the cricket match that evening—earlier that morning, Nirmila Aunty had promised to cook dinner for me and rent me whatever movie I liked. I told Kito this and he smiled.

"She'll be asleep by ten."

He dried his hands on a dish towel and asked me to meet him by the gates later, at ten; he would be waiting for me. Then he walked out of the room.

That night, Nirmila Aunty prattled on about her cousins in London, her sisters in the States, her nephews in New England, both of whom were in private schools. I felt sorry for her: she didn't have children of her own. I'd heard my parents whispering once that Rajesh Kaka was having an affair, that Nirmila Aunty was barren, that there was a child somewhere else. I wondered if this was true. She was pretty, with large dark eyes, full pink lips, slippery black hair she tied back in a bun. She was much younger than Rajesh Kaka. Once, I had heard my mother refer to her as a "tart." Still, she was kind to me, and I felt guilty about lying to her and saying I was going to read a book in my room instead of watching the movie she had rented for me at the store.

I took a steam shower and changed into fresh clothes. At nine fifty, I slipped through the back doors. The pool was glowing. The night was dark. A breeze swept through the palms. In the distance I could hear Jeeps crunching over gravel and African music streaming from an open window. I waited at the front gates for twenty minutes, but Kito never arrived. I waited ten, fifteen minutes more. Then I walked around to the back of the house. Perhaps he had asked me to meet him *there* instead. But there was no one. My heart sank. I walked back to my bedroom and, instead of slipping inside, I kept going, past the kitchen, past the patio, past the fire pit where we toasted marshmallows for s'mores, past the fence and through the servants' quarters beyond, where a small room was lit from a bare bulb.

It was there that I saw her, sitting on his bed. She was smoking. Gold hoops adorned her ears. She was pretty, with almond-shaped eyes, velvet black hair. Her mouth was very red. Moments later, Kito emerged. "What are you doing here?"

"You asked me to meet you."

I was transfixed by her: the way she held her cigarette, the way she crossed her legs, the way she sat upright and with her back against the wall, as if she had been there before. I remembered her name: Aisha. The girlfriend Kito had mentioned in a way that made her seem frivolous, extraneous even, existing separately, in a world where I did not. But she was real. Her gaze drifted slowly toward me, flashing like a gem. The room was smaller than I had imagined, with a twin bed, a metal dresser, a few of Kito's belongings scattered across the floor. Aisha stared at me, narrowing her eyes, as if she already knew everything one could know about me and was bored by it all the same. I looked at her more closely. There was a flower in her lap. I looked at her arms and saw something else: my mother's gold watch. I didn't think about it. I didn't have to. I grabbed her by the wrist. "Give that back!"

It all happened so fast. Aisha ran off into a corner of the room and Kito lunged at me, knocking me backward. "What's your problem?" His face was knotted with fury, bright with rage. He pinned me to the tiles. "You little queer," he said. "You want to hit girls?"

I shook my head.

Kito was on top of me now, straddling me like a lover, and I began to cry, softly, closing my eyes.

"Get up," he said, gently, offering me his hand.

But I pushed it away. "Don't you touch me," I hissed.

I could have stopped myself then. I could have harnessed my

rage. I could have gone back into my room and silenced the voice in my head forever.

I didn't. I said things that evening I couldn't possibly take back, vicious words that could never dwell in my heart: that Kito was a servant, a slave, and that, if he didn't apologize, I would tell everyone—Nirmila Aunty, Rajesh Kaka, even my own parents—what he had done.

There was silence. Kito stared at the floor. It was the girl, bristling with anger, who stepped forward. "Leave us," she said, in an imperious tone. "Leave us at once." She was still holding a cigarette in her hands, waving it around like a baton, when I headed for the door. It wasn't until I was on the other side of it that I heard Kito finally speak, in Swahili this time: *"Msumbufu."* Then he slammed the door.

Two days later, my parents returned with fresh tans and stories about the wildlife they had seen. Even my sister was invigorated, telling me about a leopard that had jumped in front of their car. She said it was a once-in-a-lifetime opportunity. She also said we would be leaving the next day, five days earlier than we had planned. There was a bomb threat outside the city; Nairobi had issued a curfew. My father had changed our tickets. I sat with my mother in her bedroom while she packed her bag, listening to her stories about the bush. She asked me if I had enjoyed myself and I told her I had. I didn't tell her the truth: that I had cried all day in my room, trying to decipher what Kito had whispered before closing the door: *Msumbufu*. I had never heard that word before. I watched her sort through her things: silk garments, emerald rings, a white envelope stuffed with shillings, crammed inside her purse. In the middle of it all her eyes landed on something partly hidden under her washing, flashing in front of my face. She picked it up off the floor.

"My watch," she said, triumphantly. "I've found it."

I vomited into the bushes outside.

Rajesh Kaka and Nirmila Aunty prepared a farewell feast for us, but I couldn't eat a thing. I had been hoping to catch a glimpse of Kito by the pool, swimming while everyone was taking a nap. I was hoping he would come by my room. I knocked on his door; he didn't answer it. I waited for him in the kitchen; he never showed up. I waited until nightfall but didn't see him then, either, and by morning, it became apparent that I might never see him again.

So I got an idea. I went into my mother's bedroom and found the envelope she had stuffed inside her purse, overflowing with shillings—leftover money to be divided among the staff—and knocked on Kito's door. The door swung open against the weight of my fist. The room was just as I had left it: the furnishings dusty, the bedspread wrinkled, the light murky and dim. I placed the envelope on top of Kito's dresser and waited there for a moment, as if I might discover him in the closet or by the banyans outside. Then I left the room. Years later, I would wonder why I did it. I would wonder what would have happened if Kito had been standing behind his bedroom door, waiting to receive me. Our flight wasn't until midnight, and instead of waiting around for Kito I spent the rest of the afternoon in my sister's bedroom, reading her Nancy Drew.

I heard his voice coming from the yard. I tossed the book aside and approached the bay windows and opened the curtain, watching him kick a ball around. He sprinted across the lawn to catch it as it bounced over the fire pit and landed inches away from the pool. Our eyes met. I thought he would call out to me, wave his hands in gratitude (I had assumed he was grateful for what I had done). But I was wrong. Kito stared at me blankly, scratching his head. I dropped the curtain back into place.

Later that evening, Nirmila Aunty suffocated us with hugs and kisses, smashing her breasts against our faces. She took a picture of my sister and me standing in front of the swimming pool, looking sullen. It is a picture I still have with me to this day. In it, we are wearing baseball hats and tennis shoes and our winter coats are tied in knots at our waists, as was the style. It is the only evidence I have of their house. It is the only memento from our trip. I never went back there again.

At the airport, my parents bought cookies and chocolates and red Fanta to take with us on the plane, but I was too nauseous to eat a thing. At the gate I asked my father to translate something for me, a word that still lingered in my mind. *"Msumbufu,"* I said. "What does it mean?"

He looked confused.

"It means to be a nuisance," he said.

Two days later, we returned to the States, jet-lagged and weary. My parents lined the walls with their wares: copper statues, woven mats, a wooden carving of two Maasai soldiers attached at the head. I stared at the pale crusts of snow outside our windows and longed for the greenery outside Rajesh Kaka's home. My history teacher asked me to make a presentation on my "wonderful trip to Africa," so I brought in the textiles my mother had purchased, the pictures my sister had taken, the fruits they had smuggled inside their handbags and coats. I answered my classmate's questions about the climate and the clothes. One of my classmates asked me to say something to her in Swahili. I paused, whispering it. *"Msumbufu."*

She nodded her head.

In time I threw myself into my studies, becoming the student my parents had always wanted me to be. I left the old version of myself behind in Kenya. I never looked back. I joined track and field, a sport that came rather naturally to me. I made friends, too, attending homecoming and the prom. I went to college at Duke. After graduation, I moved to the West Coast, where I started law school and where I fell in love for the first time in my life, with a third-year named Graham—a man, as it so happened to be, who would one day break my heart.

It was there that I heard the news: there had been a tragedy. A group of terrorists had invaded a large shopping center in Nairobi, setting off grenades. Nirmila Aunty had been there, along with Rajesh Kaka. Fortunately, they had survived. My mother flew back to Nairobi to be by their sides, phoning me with updates on their recovery. I remember waking up each morning with Graham, waiting to hear her voice. I remember thinking of Nirmila Aunty and Rajesh Kaka still living in Nairobi, in the middle of their middle age now, at a hospital near their home.

I did not think of Kito at all.

When she returned, my mother told me there had been a funeral: one of the houseboys was not so lucky. He had been shopping when it happened. In fact, he was my age.

"Do you remember him?" she said. "You were quite fond of him at the time."

I thought about the last time I had seen Kito in the backyard, the curtain dropping into place. It was an image I had carried with me all of those years. It wasn't until later, when I pressed my mother for details, that I realized she hadn't been referring to Kito at all.

He had left Rajesh Kaka's house years before. It had happened during our return home: Rajesh Kaka discovered a missing envelope filled with shillings in Kito's room. He had stolen from us. They fired him at once. At the time, I had assumed my mother wouldn't notice the envelope was gone. But she had, enough so to raise suspicion. She told me this with a sense of aplomb, as if it had only been a minor inconvenience. I didn't tell her the truth: that it was I who had put the envelope there in the first place. Instead, I asked her why she had never mentioned this before, why, after all those years, she had never said a word. But there was nothing left to say. By that point the vacation was over. We had returned to our lives. She had doubted, even then, that I would care. ♦

these things happen

It wasn't that I was a snob or anything; it was that Chloe wasn't the kind of girl you invited over to your house. She lived on the other side of town, where the houses were smaller, the sidewalks unswept, the cars parked in driveways instead of in the garage. I'd heard a rumor that her sister was mentally ill. We were eighteen—that sparkling age when nothing was expected of us but everything was.

"I'm a mess," she said. "But I won't stay too long. Just a couple hours and I'll be out of your hair."

Technically, I didn't invite her—my parents had gone to Australia for a couple of months, and I had thrown a party. By the time it was over, Chloe was too drunk to drive home. She was huddling over our silk sofa as if it was the gateway to heaven. I knew what she wanted.

"Just make sure you lock the door when you leave," I said.

She said nothing as I handed her a blanket and disappeared. Hours later, she was standing at my bedroom door.

"I can't sleep." She sat down beside me. "It looks like you can't sleep either."

She was wearing an Ohio State sweatshirt over cotton panties. She reached for my underwear and began sliding it down my legs.

"What are you doing?" I said.

"Nothing," she said. She placed her hand on my thigh. "I've never seen one like that before—your dick—it's different."

"It's uncircumcised."

She said nothing for a minute or two, mulling this over in her head. Then she parted her lips.

"It's beautiful."

The following Monday I was late to work. Ray was waiting for me in the kitchen.

He was the assistant manager of IHOP and he acted like it was the most important thing in the world. Sometimes he would give me a shove or a kick and I would have to pretend that it didn't happen—that it was all part of the job.

"There are plenty of people who want this job," he warned.

"No one wants this job," I said. "Even *you* don't want this job."

He told me to watch my fucking mouth and get back to work. Then he disappeared. I washed up in the basin—which was littered with cigarette butts, pancake batter, globs of cinnamon raisin oatmeal. My first customer stared at the menu like it was written in Chinese.

"Now let's see," she said. "Does the short stack come with bacon?"

There was a flash of movement across the room; someone was waving at me. I turned my head. It was Chloe. She wasn't alone; there was a pretty girl sitting across from her looking painfully bored.

"What are you doing here?" I said, abandoning the customer and walking over to Chloe's table.

"I'm eating. What does it look like I'm doing?"

I grabbed an empty soup bowl and walked over to the kitchen; a few moments later, I returned. "Did you know I work here?"

"Of course, dummy. It's why I came."

"Why?"

"Because I wanted to talk to you."

"About what?"

"About the weather—Jesus—I don't know. Why haven't you called?"

At this moment, Chloe's companion dropped her fork onto her plate and rolled her eyes.

"My sister is mad at you because you fucked her and never called."

I felt myself go red. A woman turned to stare at us and I quickly smiled back at her, reassuringly.

"Keep your voice down."

The sister looked as though she found the whole thing utterly comical. She doused her plate with syrup and resumed eating. I watched her silently. She wore an over-the-shoulder sweater, large gold earrings. Her hair was a cinnamon shade of brown. On her wrist was a series of bangles and a plastic bracelet with her name on it—Tara Evans—followed by a bar code. She caught me staring at it and clucked her tongue.

"What?" she said. "Never seen a mental patient before?"

Work the next day was the usual: old women with frosted hair, college kids in colored jerseys, families with their screaming kids. The whole place smelled like coffee and smoke.

"You're on cleanup duty," Ray said. "Now stop fucking around."

Cleanup consisted of washing dishes and hosing down vats

full of bacon grease. I smoked a few joints instead. When my shift was over, I walked out to the parking lot and discovered Tara leaning against my car.

"Hi."

"Hi," I said.

"My sister is in love with you. You know that, right?"

I shrugged. She offered me a cigarette and I took it from her. I looked for the name tag on her wrist but it was gone.

"Are you really a mental patient?"

She smiled. "Are you asking if I'm crazy?"

She was wearing a black tank top over jeans. She was sweating. There were charcoal patches of mascara beneath her eyes. "This town is bloody boring," she said, in a fake British accent. "More boring than I recalled."

"My father says it's good to be bored."

"Your father is crazier than I am."

I wondered if this was true.

"So *are* you?"

"Am I what?"

"A mental patient."

She shrugged. The heat shimmered; sunlight dappled her face. She cut her eyes up to mine.

"I want to see where you live."

We drove in my father's Mercedes, listening to Rage Against The Machine. Tara changed the station.

"This is shit," she said. "My bloody ears are on fire."

I wondered if Tara really was British. I wondered if she was adopted. Maybe that's why she was crazy. There was a girl from our neighborhood who was adopted by two retinal surgeons; her name was Melissa and she was very fat. She looked nothing like her slender parents. Once, when we were little, Melissa marched over to me and lifted up her dress.

This is my no-no.

I had never heard of a *no-no* before, but then Melissa pulled her panties off and began dancing around.

No, no, no, she sang. *No one can touch my no-no. No one but me!*

I touched it anyways.

The next evening, when Melissa invited me over to watch *The Little Mermaid* in her parents' basement, I touched it again.

By the time we reached my house the sun was impossibly high; the lake was like tinfoil. Tara glanced around.

"I figured it would be like this."

She stared at the expensive tapestries, the cream-colored walls, the Hindu statues with their multitude of arms. She picked one of them up in her hands. "What's this?" she said, smiling.

It was the goddess Kali. It was frightening looking. My parents had bought it in India—along with other frightening things. I was embarrassed by it, but Tara shook her head.

"It's beautiful."

"What?"

"It's feminist, Venkat. I want it—I want it for my room."

I wondered what a room in a mental ward was like—I pictured a padded white cell with metal bars on the windows. Tara put the statue down and gave me a look.

"Got any weed?"

We smoked outside. After three hits I was gone, blinded by the sheen of Tara's legs. I hadn't even noticed that she had taken off her clothes. She was wading through our swimming pool in her panties and bra.

"Get in," she said. "The water feels amazing."

I watched her like a shark. She watched me back. Her hair was flaxen, fanned out like a jellyfish. Her eyes were liquid green. In the sparkling light she smiled at me.

"You're high."

"No, I'm not." I giggled. "I'm not."

"You are. Prove it."

I undid my pants, sliding them down to my feet. I peeled off my T-shirt and jumped right in. The water was cold, freezing my spine and making my nipples shrink like raisins. Tara swam over to me immediately.

"You're cute."

She slipped her hands into my shorts, rubbing the tip of my cock. I was harder than hell. When she pulled away, there were little rivulets of mascara running down her cheeks.

"You could fuck me, you know," she said, kissing my lips, my chin, the dark hair on my chest. Then she drifted away. She stepped out of the pool, water sluicing off her legs.

By the time I turned around she was gone.

That night, I drank two Jack and Cokes and watched a marathon of *Mad Men* on TV. I thought about my parents. They had emailed me from Australia, where my father had gone snorkeling on the Great Barrier Reef. My emails back to them were full of lies, stories about school, about a math exam I had taken and how I had gotten the highest grade—in reality I had missed the exam, and my math teacher, Mrs. Beaumont, had left three messages on my parents' machine. On Sunday morning I slept through my alarm, skipping my shift at work, and at ten thirty Chloe called.

"You're making a huge mistake."

"What?"

"My sister—I know you've been seeing her."

"So?"

"So she's crazy."

The light outside my room was blinding. I got out of bed.

"She lies, you know. One time, she told my parents she was teaching English abroad and then later we found out she was working at a diner in Illinois." She paused. "And then there's the other stuff."

"What other stuff?"

I went downstairs. The kitchen was in disarray. There was a box of dried-up, half-eaten pizza on the stove.

"I'll tell you later," Chloe said.

"You'll tell me now."

"I'll tell you in person. When can you meet?"

"What for?" I said, growing impatient. "What do you want from me, anyways? What's *wrong* with you?"

The next day I looked out for Tara but there was no sign of her. I waited for her in the parking lot but she never came. I circled the IHOP and drove by her house and after stalling for twenty minutes I drove back home. I lit up a joint. Chloe called six times that evening. *I need to talk to you.* She left voicemails I deleted, sent text messages I ignored. She wrote emails with the subject heading "please read now." I discarded each one. After a few days of this, I blocked her number altogether. I started drinking again, a few Jacks here and there; sometimes it was so much I couldn't remember where I was. Once, I swallowed a handful of molly and woke up hours later in my parents' garage. The phone rang and I answered it. It was Tara.

"Let's hang."

The first time we fucked it was raining: one of those cool autumn rains that soak through your skin. The streets were slick and glistening and the clouds were like clumps of steel wool. Tara was aggressive in bed.

"I like it this way," she said. "And from behind."

She visited me at work, planting herself in the back, reading thick yellow novels by Russian authors she loved. She wore the same three T-shirts with flared skirts. Her arms, long and thin, were covered in bracelets. She never took them off. I didn't know what Tara did; she'd spent a year in college before declaring it a doomed enterprise, a waste of her intellect. Then she went crazy. I didn't know about her past, about the mental wellness facility or why she was there, but then one day she took off her bracelets—gold, pink, silver, blue—and showed me the scars.

She said the first cut was scary in the way most good things seem scary at first—like diving off a cliff or a bridge. But the fear quickly changed into something else. Something she couldn't describe. It had happened in college, during the spring of her freshman year, and her roommate had found her lying on the floor.

"My parents didn't know what to do with me," she said. "And I didn't have anywhere else to go."

We became entwined like those trees in the forest that bind together to form one giant tree. I continued to skip school, a result of Tara's exhortations, and the messages mounted on my parents' machine. We had picnics at my house, feeding each other with our hands. We kissed for hours in the back row of foreign films. Sometimes we would get drunk and go to the park and play on the swing set and gaze up at the stars. Once, Tara showed up at my work wearing a trench coat.

"I'm naked underneath."

We fucked in the backseat of my car. In the moonlight Tara's raised scars looked like streaks of mother-of-pearl. She asked me to kiss them and I did.

"It feels the same," she said, shivering. "It feels just like before."

I told her I felt it, too. Then one evening, I was alone in the kitchen when I started thinking about Melissa and *The Little Mermaid*. I don't know why. Maybe it was one of those things: one thought follows another, naturally. I wiped the image from my mind. I called Tara. Later that evening, we were drinking absinthe by the pool.

"What's it like?" I said.

"What?"

"That place—the one where you used to live."

"The loony bin?" She laughed. She was wearing a leather jacket and denim shorts. She was shivering. "It's like summer camp," she said. "Except that everyone's crazy. And the counselors have Ph.D.s. And every morning you have to fill out these stupid questionnaires." She lit a cigarette in her hands. "And no one writes to you. Your parents stop pretending you exist. They visit you every now and again but never ask you how you are."

"My parents do that anyways," I said. "That doesn't sound so bad."

"It's worse." Tara shook her head. "It's like being in a zoo. But it doesn't matter, anyways, because I'm never going back."

She walked over to where I was sitting and kissed me openly on the mouth. Then she sat on my lap. We stayed like that for a while, Tara and I, until the sky bled purple and orange and pink. Later that morning, I told her I loved her.

It was like that for a while: sex and talking, talking and sex. We never went to Tara's house; instead she slept over at mine. I figured she was embarrassed about where she lived—once, Tara had asked me what my parents did for a living, and, when I told her my father was a cardiologist, she had made a snide remark. And then there was Chloe. She still emailed me from time to time. She called from private numbers. Once we saw her car parked outside my garage.

"And *I'm* the crazy one," Tara said.

It was gone by morning. Tara made French toast with caramelized bananas and we ate them in my parents' bed. Her dream was to study pastry in New York, open a bakery of her own. When she asked me what *my* dreams were I didn't know what to say.

"A boy without a dream?" She began kissing me all over. "Now that's the saddest thing I ever heard."

Then one day, Tara disappeared. It was seven o'clock; we had planned to meet at the park. The sun was setting and the sky had turned the color of blood. I was sitting under a tree, watching a group of teenagers playing touch football near the swings, when I began to lose hope. I called Tara's cell phone; there was no answer. I sent her a text message. There was no reply. The sun dipped behind the trees like bright molten lava. I smoked a cigarette and left.

I ate Cheerios in front of the TV all the next day and waited for Tara to call—she didn't. I went to her house and she wasn't there. I waited three more days and heard nothing. Then I drove to school.

She was standing by her locker, a smile on her face. When she saw me approaching the smile quickly vanished.

"Where is she?" I said.

"Who?"

"Tara. Where did she go?"

She said nothing.

"Where, Chloe?"

She let her purse slip from her hands. "I called you—I called you about a million times. I sent you text messages. Emails. I thought maybe you were dead or something. You could have just told me to get lost."

"I've been busy."

She shook her head. "Well, you won't be *busy* anymore. She's gone, you know—Tara. You won't be seeing her again."

"What do you mean she's gone? Where did she go?"

"Why should I tell *you*?"

"Because I'm her friend, that's why. I have a right to know."

"Her *friend*." Chloe laughed. "Tara doesn't have friends. She doesn't stick around long enough to make them."

I could see it in her eyes: the smugness. I wondered what would happen if I punched her in the face. I remembered how she had snuck into my bedroom that night and done what she did. "You're wasting your time," Chloe said, packing up her things. "But I think you realize that by now." She stood back and shook her hair and I caught a whiff of her bodywash or her shampoo. "She's back in the hospital," she said, giving me a look I would never forget. "She cut herself again."

At the hospital, I was greeted by a short black woman sitting at an information desk lined with silver frames.

"I'm here to see Tara Evans."

"Who?"

"Tara Evans. She's on the psychiatric floor."

She glanced at her computer. A family rushed by carrying silver balloons. I was reminded of the time my father took me to the hospital, seating me in the doctors' lounge, handing me a stethoscope in hopes that I would become a doctor as well. I remembered the day we drove four hours to visit Ohio State University. I was only twelve at the time, but I had roamed the campus anyways, sipping coffee on the quad, and after dinner my father gave me my first taste of beer. The next morning, there was an application for the six-year medical program at Ohio State University sitting on my desk at home. I pinned it to my wall. I knew what was expected of me. I knew what he wanted. There was never any question of that.

A few minutes passed and the woman looked up at me with a frown.

"I'm afraid the patient is no longer here."

"What?"

"She checked out this morning."

"Where did she go?"

"She's been transferred."

"Transferred where?"

"She's been transferred to Graves," the woman said. "The mental wellness facility."

For three days I sat by the pool, drinking cheap wine. I got fired from the IHOP. I called Tara's cell phone about a million times. Then one day I got an email from her. It said that she was sorry, that she didn't mean for it to happen, that she loved me and that if I loved her back I would find her—if I had the time.

It was all I needed to hear.

The facility was sixty miles away, in a town I had never seen. It was nicer than I had expected. The walls were made of glass and steel. A woman with sculpted blond hair told me to sign in—

visiting hours were just beginning—then directed me to a waiting room out back. There were other visitors: women in business suits, grandmothers with their dogs, young girls wearing tank tops over name-brand jeans. They looked nothing like I had imagined. The facility, with its antiseptic gleam, looked nothing like I had imagined. And then I realized something: Tara's family weren't who I thought they were. I took a seat by the windows. I stretched out my legs. I glanced at the coffee table and picked up a magazine. The cover featured a pretty young girl standing in a field with a question mark floating above her head: "Do I belong?"

"No," I whispered, turning the page. "You do not."

Moments later, a woman in a white coat led us down a hall. My stomach began to turn. I thought about that night in my car, the dazed look on Tara's face. I thought about Melissa, too. It had been years since it had happened, but the memory was still fresh in my mind. It was her parents who'd caught us. We were in Melissa's basement, on a bed reserved for visitors, in a corner of the room we hadn't thought they would look in. "Sex-play" is what they called it. This was what they explained to my parents that evening, sheepish yet calm, their smiles frozen beneath designer frames. They said it was perfectly natural: these things happen. But only I knew the truth. Only I knew what I had done to her. Years later, I could still hear her cries. I could still feel her rigid body beneath my frame. I realized that this was what Tara noticed when she saw me that first day at the IHOP, and the day after that, in the parking lot.

I realized we were the same.

The woman in the white coat opened the door and everyone filed into a room—mothers, daughters—everyone but me. I stood outside and waited. I shifted my feet. I swallowed the lump of coal that had lodged itself in my throat. I peered into the room. Tara was sitting with her arms folded across her chest. She was staring at the wall. I could almost hear her breathing. Earlier that morning, the secretary had told me that Tara was expecting my visit and that it was nice to see someone show some initiative for a change.

She never saw me leave. I never saw her again. By the time I reached home, the clouds were gray and the rain fell harder than I had ever felt it before, lashing my skin. I can think of one time afterward when it rained that hard. The time I saw Chloe. It was the Saturday after homecoming, and I was drunk at a bar. Chloe was with her friends. She spent the whole evening giving me weird looks from afar, until finally, just as I was leaving, she reached for my hand.

"Take me home."

I did as I was told. By the time we reached Chloe's house my pants were around my ankles and we were fucking in the back-seat of my car, as if nothing had ever happened. Two days later, I got a letter in the mail. It was from the six-year medical program at Ohio State University. It was a letter of regret. I took it inside. I placed it on the stove. I poured myself a whiskey and went searching for a knife. Then I took the knife onto my parents' patio and locked the door. For an hour I did nothing. It was not Chloe who saved me, or my neighbor, Mrs. Williams, but my parents, returning home from their vacation, prying the knife from my hands. ♦

an arrangement

I never wanted to marry Akhil. My mother found his picture on a website I had never heard of (and to which I unwittingly belonged). He was an anesthesiologist. He was a graduate of Yale. We were married in a small ceremony outside of Skokie, Illinois. On the day of our wedding, I wore my mother's silk sari and her diamond-studded choker with rubies and pearls.

I didn't know him very well. He was cute in a way. His arms were corded with muscle. His thick dark hair was flecked with gray. Sometimes he would do something—bite his lips, flex his arms—and I would want to rip off his clothes. But then the moment would pass. We made love sparingly, at night usually, with Akhil on top. It was a life, I guess.

We moved to Chicago, where Akhil started a practice in pain management and I got a job at a prestigious law firm downtown. We made friends, too. Sometimes I would pretend to like one of them—then go home at night and complain to Akhil:

"What a bitch."

He never said a word. He didn't say much at all, really. Once, I went shopping at Saks Fifth Avenue and spent half our mortgage on a pair of shoes. Afterward I tried hiding the bill. A month passed and then two and then one night we were at dinner with the chief of medical staff when our credit card was declined.

"That's strange."

He pulled out another one. Later, he checked the statement online.

"Looks like we never got a bill."

The first time we tried to get pregnant, I went to CVS and bought a package of Plan B.

"It's your sperm," I told him. "It's not strong enough. You're not a strong enough man."

He made an appointment with the gynecologist. I canceled it. A woman? I didn't want her anywhere near my parts.

"I don't want her touching me there," I said.

After a few months of this we put the baby on hold.

"It's Akhil," I told my parents, crying to them over the phone. "He won't touch me anymore."

It was like this for a while. I pushed his buttons on purpose. Then one evening, I came home to find a bassinet sitting in the corner of our living room.

"For when the baby arrives."

I dropped my briefcase on the floor.

"Where did you find it?"

"At Macy's, on my way back from work. I thought you would enjoy it."

I stared at him.

"But you can't even get me pregnant."

He packed it away. I expected him to shout at me or to scream, but as usual he took the derision in stride, saying nothing at all.

The next morning, we made love in our usual way: for twenty minutes, or until one of us got bored. Then he kissed me on the forehead and went straight to the gym.

I should have known there was someone else. I discovered it one evening after a party: a napkin fell out of his pocket containing a phone number written in bright red lipstick, next to a name. Celine. I put the napkin back into his pocket. I wanted him to have it. I don't know why. All week long I waited for his betrayal: a whispered phone call, a canceled plan, the scent of another woman's perfume. But nothing happened. Then one evening, I was tidying up in the bedroom when I found the napkin pressed into Akhil's textbook, quietly preserved. The lipstick had smeared. But the number was still there. I went into the kitchen and dialed it.

"Is this Celine?"

She hesitated a moment before saying, "Yes."

"Oh, hi," I said. "This is Rupa—Rupa Varma."

I poured myself a drink from the bar.

"Akhil's wife."

She hung up the phone.

That night, I cooked lamb curry and set the table for two. Akhil came home with a bottle of wine. Together we drank it over a platter of crackers and cheese.

"I talked to Celine," I said.

"Who?"

"Celine—your mistress."

He took a sip of his wine. A piece of cheese fell out of his hands and he picked it back up, slowly.

"Don't be silly. I don't know what you mean."

"You don't be silly," I said, the wine blooming. I put the napkin in front of him.

"See? She gave you her number. She wants you to call. I thought we could be friends but she hung up the phone—how rude."

The rice cooker clicked and I scooped a steaming spoonful of rice onto his plate. Then I went into the kitchen. After dinner, Akhil rinsed the dishes and put them in the dishwasher and began wiping the counters off with a rag.

"She's a pharmaceutical representative," he said, before retiring to bed. "She didn't have her card."

He was right: I found Celine's LinkedIn page online. I was hoping to find a picture of her, too. But there was nothing. In my mind Celine had the kind of bright blond hair that made girls in high school want to kill themselves. She had long legs, too. Probably she was skinny and probably she wore silk blouses over the swell of her breasts. I went home that evening and called her again.

"It's me," I said. "Rupa Varma."

"What do you want?"

"I want to know what the hell you're doing with my husband."

I sat in the living room with the television on mute, vague images flashing over my face. I could hear music on the other end. She was silent a moment, as if she hadn't heard the question. Then she spoke abruptly, in a voice that was stilted and clear.

"I'm his friend."

"What kind of friend?"

She didn't answer me. I could hear the sound of liquid crackling over ice; she was pouring herself a drink.

Then she replied, very softly, "I've given him something you won't."

"A blow job?"

She laughed.

"An arrangement."

"What kind of arrangement?"

"A special one."

"But he's married."

She hung up the phone. I dialed her number, but there was no answer. I dialed it again. Then I sent her a nasty text message. I waited for Akhil to come home, and when he didn't, I fell asleep on the couch; then I crawled into our bedroom. The next morning, he wasn't in our bed.

"Akhil?" I said, checking the bathroom and the den. "Akhil?"

I went downstairs and found the doorman, Raul.

"Where is Akhil?"

"I haven't seen him, miss. Not since yesterday morning."

I went back upstairs. Hours later, Akhil came home with Chinese takeaway from the restaurant down the road.

"Where were you?"

I was wearing sweat socks and leggings. My eyes were smeared with mascara. I was holding a glass of sherry.

"I was on call," Akhil said. "You know that."

"Liar."

He went into the kitchen and opened the cupboards, looking for a pot or a pan. Then he spun around.

"Are you hungry?"

"You were with that whore, weren't you?"

He was silent. "I told you, she's a pharmaceutical representative."

The next evening we had a fight: something about the way he looked at me sent me flying into a rage.

"Don't you look at me that way," I said.

I'd spent the entire evening drinking red wine on the sofa, watching soap operas on TV. I'd discovered a lump in my breast. It was nothing, really; my breasts had always been lumpy. Still, I couldn't help but imagine myself bald.

"You didn't go to work today," he said. "You haven't been to work all week."

"I was bored."

"They'll fire you."

"Good."

"Good?" He arched his brow. "And then what? How will we afford to pay for this loft? How will you afford to buy those five-hundred-dollar shoes?"

"I'll sue."

"Sue for what?"

"For sexual harassment," I said. "For all the leers and the stares. You should see the way they look at me over there: like they're all screwing me in their heads."

"Don't be ridiculous."

He didn't come home for three nights that week. I spent my evenings on the sofa, watching reality TV. I wondered if he was with Celine. Probably he was. Probably they were in some dark bar with snifters and smoke. Probably they were screwing in the backseat of a cab.

I woke up one morning and called her again. She didn't answer, but later, at work, I found her Facebook profile online. She was pretty but not in the way I had imagined: Her hair wasn't blond; it was dark and moist and curly. She looked vaguely African

American. There were a few pictures and in each of them she looked the same: bright-eyed, smiling, as if she knew I was watching. There was one in particular that I liked. She was standing at a bar in a gold sequined dress. A man stood behind her with his hand on her breast. It was a picture that spoke of perversion or cruelty, or perhaps it was an innocent consequence of drinking too much the night before. I downloaded the picture onto my computer. Then I left work for the day.

That night, Akhil was late again, but I didn't bother asking him where he'd been. I ate my dinner on the sofa and went straight to the den. I found the picture again. It flickered brightly—different, but the same, in the way an ex-lover's face can seem different, but the same. Only this time she wasn't looking at me at all. This time, her gaze had drifted elsewhere, as if I now bored her.

I called her the next day.

"It's me: Rupa Varma."

"Look, I told you: I'm not getting involved."

"But you are involved."

I was dressed in a business suit. Akhil was in the shower. The apartment windows were streaked with morning light.

"I'm pregnant," I blurted.

She was silent.

"So it's important that you stop seeing him. It's important that you leave us alone. Do you understand?"

She said nothing.

"We have a child together—a child—and you're coming between us. Is that the sort of woman you want to be? The sort of woman who comes between a father and his child?"

I thought she would tell me to get lost or hang up the phone or threaten to call the police.

Instead she gave me her address.

"Meet me at five thirty," she said. "And come alone."

All morning I was jittery. I drank three cups of coffee. I ate a jelly donut. I went across the street for a glass of champagne. I couldn't concentrate on my work. I crawled underneath my desk and took an afternoon nap. Pretty soon it was five and by then it seemed likely that five thirty would never arrive. When it finally approached, I closed my laptop and left work for the day.

Celine lived in a dark neighborhood lined with restaurants and bars. I had expected something different. In my mind she lived in a condominium with a doorman and a pool. I was wrong. When the cab pulled up to her town house I saw a rusted Dodge in the driveway. The house was tall and crumbling, with sheer white curtains above. There was a wraparound porch with a bench and a swing. I rang the doorbell. She answered it. Moments later, it started to rain.

"Come in."

She looked different from her pictures—she was still pretty, but in a different way. Her face was slimmer. Her house was crammed with junk, too: jade statues and thick books on art and sex and food. There were pictures of her and some woman who looked just like her all over the walls, a sister perhaps, maybe even a twin. I wondered if Akhil had been here. I wondered if he had left something behind: a pair of shoes or a hat or something else I would recognize. But there was nothing. Celine led me into her living room, with its beige rug and its soiled chairs and its dusty bookcases that covered the entire length of the wall. She pulled up a chair.

"When are you due?"

"What?"

She looked panicked suddenly, her eyes growing wide. "He said you couldn't get pregnant," she said. "He said you were getting a divorce. That was part of the deal."

I said nothing. Finally she went into the kitchen and came back with a pot of tea.

"Would you like some?"

"Sure."

We sat in silence, stirring our tea, the rain drumming against the leaves. Then she put her teacup aside and folded her arms.

"I take it he didn't tell you. I take it you don't know. He told me you did. He said I shouldn't worry, that you're not well." She paused, staring. "But you don't seem all that unwell to *me*—and now you're pregnant."

I didn't tell her I was lying. My eyes landed on a picture of Celine with her arms wrapped around another woman, the same woman from before. The sister.

"That's my lover, Claire. She'll be the one to carry it."

"Carry what?"

"The baby," she said.

I dropped my saucer onto the carpet.

"Of course I'll be in charge of the insemination. He'll have no part in that. But we did agree to let him be a part of the child's life, to be the father in practice and in name, and there's the biology, too—I mean, it won't technically be mine."

I began to feel dizzy.

"He didn't tell you this?" she asked. "He said you didn't want a child. He said you were barren. I mean a doctor, a graduate of Yale, we couldn't pass up the chance." She paused, dropping a cube of sugar into her tea. Then she leaned in and whispered, "He offered me some money, too, but of course I refused."

She was lying—I could see it in her eyes. I bolted for the door.

"Where are you going?"

I ran outside, hailing a cab, instructing the driver to make a left at the curb. I closed my eyes. I kept them closed the entire way home until finally we were sitting in front of my lobby, the rain dribbling to a halt. Then I opened them again.

"That'll be twenty dollars, miss."

That evening, I saw her everywhere: in the reflection of the shower, in the shadows of the hall, even in my dreams. *Where are you going?* It was maddening. I couldn't shake her from my mind. I kept seeing those wild green eyes and that glossy mane of hair. I kept hearing her name, too: Celine, like the whisper in a breeze.

I never called her again. I didn't have to. Three days later, she left me an angry voicemail.

"I haven't heard from you. You never called. You better not ruin this for us—that baby is ours."

I didn't tell anyone about it—not because I was sad or scared but because by then I had begun to believe her a little. I don't know why. She could have been anyone, really: a lunatic, a crazy person, someone who invented things the way crazy people did. Still, I was careful. I got pregnant six weeks later during a weekend trip to Tulum, when Akhil and I were celebrating his fortieth birthday. I made sure of it. He was drunk and a little stoned when I led him upstairs and asked him if he was ready, and later, when he wrapped his legs around me, telling me that he was.

Or maybe he wasn't. Two years later, I ran into Celine at a hair salon with a BabyBjörn and a baby who looked an awful lot like Akhil. "Excuse me," I said, walking over to her. "How could this happen?" She raised her hands, backing away from the door. After a few moments she bolted out of the room. I followed her outside but by then it was too late: she had already disappeared. Out of the parking lot. Out of our lives for good. ♦

world famous

When I didn't match, I went home to Illinois and became one of those ghosts you saw at the mall: the ones who never left. My parents were at my sister's house in Seattle for the summer; she had just had a baby boy. The baby's name, Rohan, was a link between two worlds, Indian and Gaelic. Rohan was both, with soft, golden skin. I'd met him days after his birth. "Stay," my sister had said, her eyes rimmed with fatigue. "Spend the summer with us. What are you going to do all by yourself in Illinois?" My parents agreed. I pitied their pity.

I flew home instead, watching over their house. I answered the telephone the few times it rang in the night. "They're in Seattle," I said. "Yes, yes. It's wonderful news." The house was unnervingly still. It was a two-story brick structure my father had built for us when I was ten. He was a doctor himself, but he no longer practiced. He owned a clinic and employed other doctors to practice in his place.

"Never work for anyone," he would say, after one too many beers. "Everyone is an asshole."

When I called to tell him the news—that I hadn't matched—my father had gone quiet over the phone. I had expected him to berate me, but what he said instead was much worse.

"Well, what can you do?"

What can you do? It was the finality that so unnerved me: there was nothing that could be done.

My mother behaved like a publicist.

"No need to tell anyone. What business is it of theirs, anyway? Sharmila Aunty will have questions, I'm sure. But don't worry: I will handle her."

Later, I overheard my mother telling Sharmila Aunty that I had taken the year off to do research.

So it was settled. The dust cleared. My parents could show their faces in public again. Then my sister had the baby and they flew to Seattle, no longer needing to.

The first few days at their house were strange. I kept hearing odd noises downstairs. The white carpets retained the imprints of a vacuum cleaner. The granite surfaces were polished and slick. The rooms, bright and spacious, were empty. I stared out the windows and caught a glimpse of our neighbor, Mrs. Kenyon, fetching the newspaper in her robe. Cars flicked by the cul-de-sac and I saw the glint of their wheels. My cell phone pierced the silence and I awakened from a nap, coated in sweat.

I drank steadily, whole bottles of whiskey and scotch. Blue-faced gods looked on in disapproval. In school, my teacher, Mrs. Nussbaum, had asked me to make a presentation on Hinduism. She had wanted to know more about my "culture." We were studying world religions, and, after Jennifer Goldberg talked about Hanukkah, it was my turn. "Encore," she said, "I'd like you to teach the class about Diwali."

My name is Ankur. But it was easier to let everyone call me Encore. After a few years of this, I started saying it myself. "Hi," I once said to an Indian classmate in college. "I'm Encore." She looked surprised. Later, she told me her name was Anupuma Vandhana Narayanaswami.

On my third night at home, I went through my high school yearbook. I was twenty-eight, two months shy of our ten-year reunion. The images of my classmates were younger versions of the ones I'd seen recently on Facebook. I found my senior picture, remembering the sunny afternoon when I had had it taken. It was three weeks before the start of senior year, and my hair was bleached from the sun; a diamond shone in my ear. I was staring at that earring, feeling around for the faint depression it had left behind, when I noticed her face.

At school, everyone had assumed that Anjali and I were related. Some people thought we were dating. A few others said it was both. "Encore and Angelica are having a two-headed baby."

She was a shy, quiet girl who kept mostly to herself. Her hair was the texture of wool. Acne scars formed dark pits on her cheeks. I felt sorry for her, remembering the times she had turned bright red when our teacher called on her in class. She was the daughter of family friends, people my parents socialized with at parties but kept at a distance—they weren't rich like we were. Anjali's father owned a motel. He drove a Camry. He wore brown dress pants and white tennis shoes, and his hair gleamed with coconut oil.

At those parties, Anjali traded her stonewashed denim for *lenghas* or *shalwars.* She had a sense of humor, a startling laugh I never heard in the hallways at school. She was friends with other Indian girls who lived in neighboring towns. They giggled while braiding each other's hair, or choreographing dances to Bollywood songs. Sometimes they performed these dances in the basement of someone's home, and I, their faithful audience, watched them. In those moments, Anjali came to life, swinging her hips, batting her eyes. Crowds gathered at weddings and Diwali parties just to watch her. Uncles whistled while Anjali spun in circles, her belly, exposed beneath the jeweled hem of her blouse, glistening with sweat. I often wondered what happened to her on Monday mornings when she walked into class with a blank expression on her face. We didn't talk much at school. We were the only Indians in our class; there was no need to make it more obvious.

I put away the yearbook and remembered what my parents had told me about Anjali: that her marriage to a man named Vijay had ended one year after the wedding. It was a community scandal. My parents had been invited to that wedding. So had I. I didn't attend: I was a second-year medical student, wrapped up in my exams. I hardly remembered her. Little was revealed as to why the marriage had ended. Anjali's parents simply called everyone to tell them the news: the relationship was over. But my parents and their friends speculated. Some said Anjali had a drinking problem. Others said the groom, Vijay, was from a wealthy family, and that Anjali's parents couldn't afford to keep up. Still others said it was a consequence of life in America, that kids just did as they pleased.

The next morning, I went for a run in the neighborhood and found Dr. Bernstein watering his plants.

"Ankur," he said, walking over to me. "I didn't expect to see you here. You're in medical school, right?"

He wore a white T-shirt over navy shorts. His hair, thinning at the crown, clung to his scalp.

"I just graduated," I said.

He smiled. Dr. Bernstein's house had Corinthian columns. The shrubs were perfectly trimmed. He was a colleague of my father's, and he had invited us to dinner throughout the years, though my mother had always complained: "I can't eat that bland food."

"So what's the plan now?"

I told him what had happened. I wasn't ashamed: Dr. Bernstein's son, Seth, worked at Target. He was a college dropout. He played in a band. I remember my mother coming home one evening after seeing the Bernsteins at a hospital function, appalled.

"You won't believe," she said. "You won't believe the way Susan went on about Seth, as if he is world famous." She gestured with her hand. "What rubbish. Can you be happy with a son like that?" Later, she made sure to tell me that if I ever did something like that, she would die.

"How's Seth?"

Dr. Bernstein's face darkened. "Seth is okay," he said. "He's in therapy. We're just grateful he's home. Let's be thankful for that."

I didn't know Seth was in therapy. I remembered him as an outgoing child, inviting me to shoot hoops with him after school. I couldn't help but imagine what my mother would have said if I were in therapy, too.

"We'll tell everyone you fell and broke your head."

Three months before, when I had gotten the news that I hadn't matched, I drank two forties and punched a hole in my wall. No one could explain it. My board scores were high. My interviews went well. It was one of those freak things. The match was like a lottery: you chose what residency you wanted and where, then some mysterious process handled the rest. Most people got what they wanted: OB, Family, Internal. But a few of us were left behind. Some people "scrambled," setting aside their pride to join programs in undesirable states. I went home and sulked.

One night, I got bored and went to a bar. The bar was empty, so I played on my phone for a while, checking Facebook and Instagram, until I noticed an attractive woman walk into the room. She wore a low-cut blouse of black fabric. Her skin shone like amber. Dark hair bounced at her shoulders. Something stirred inside me. I hadn't been with a woman in months. In medical school, I'd dated a Persian girl named Shanaz. After the match, I'd gotten drunk and showed up at Shanaz's front door, but she wasn't home, so I went to a bar and picked up a white girl instead.

"Can I get you anything?" the bartender asked.

I ordered a beer and played it cool for a while, scrolling through a bunch of Shanaz's old pictures on Instagram. When I looked up from the table, the woman was gone.

"Here you go," the bartender said.

He deposited the beer and walked away. A group of college students came in. They started screaming at one another and ordering a round of shots. Had I ever been that obnoxious? I was about to put some cash down and call it a night when I felt the air stir behind me.

I spun around.

The woman's blouse was silver, not black. She smelled of perfume. She was much younger looking up close. All that makeup had been a ruse. I was about to ask her who she was when it dawned on me. I should have known all along.

"Ankur, right?" she said. "I thought it was you. I was just thinking to myself: Is that Ankur Patel?"

The last time I had seen Anjali was at a wedding, shortly after high school graduation. She looked completely different now. Her hair was slicked straight. The acne marks were gone. She leaned in to give me a hug and I felt the damp surface of her skin.

"I had no idea it was you," I said.

Had I been staring at her inappropriately? I offered her a drink.

"Dirty martini."

I remembered what my parents had said, that Anjali had a drinking problem. I ordered the martini.

"Are you visiting family?" she asked.

"Sort of."

"Well, I live here," she said, sitting next to me. "But I'm sure you've already heard."

My expression must have changed, because she put her hand on my arm.

"It's okay," she said, laughing. "It's not like it's a secret. Everyone knows about the marriage that never was."

The martini came and Anjali carefully plucked the olive from its toothpick and popped it into her mouth.

"I guess you get tired of hearing about it," I said.

"Actually," she replied, chewing, "I think it's kind of funny."

"You do?"

She stared at me. "You're aware of what happened, aren't you?"

I shook my head.

"He was gay."

"Your husband?"

"Yeah."

"How did you find out?"

She frowned.

"I found some websites in his browsing history—and there was the sex. After a while, you have to wonder why you haven't had it yet. His parents were desperate to get him married." She finished her martini in a single gulp. "And now I know why."

Perhaps it was the alcohol, or the circumstance of our meeting, but we were able to open up to each other in a way we never had before. I couldn't reconcile the Anjali I had known before—the girl who avoided eye contact at every turn—with this new woman before me. She was candid, explaining that she hadn't been in a relationship with anyone in years.

"The worst part about all of this is the gossip. When you get divorced, everything from your marriage comes spilling out."

"Like what?" I asked, boldly.

She shook her head. "It's not important." She asked me what I was doing in town and I told her the truth. "Wow," she said, tapping her glass against mine. "We're the talk of the town."

We went home separately that night, but the next day, I thought about Anjali all afternoon. I went on Facebook and found her profile. Her pictures were recent, blurred snapshots of herself at bars. Her pose was always the same: her head tilted, her hand on her hip, her lips parted, revealing a chunk of white teeth. I spent nearly an hour clicking past each one, until I got to an old picture of Anjali from years ago. It was taken at a party my parents had thrown when I was twelve. The memory of that evening flashed through my mind like a dream. Families from all over crowded our living room, eating curry out of Styrofoam trays. The women wore silk saris. The men wore dress shirts and slacks.

Anjali wore a peach *lengha,* with pink and purple jewels. My father played "Jumma Chumma De De" on our stereo system, bouncing his shoulders like Amitabh Bachchan in the movie *Hum*. I had seen that movie and laughed. "It's not even him singing," I'd said. "How can you watch this crap?" Halfway into the song, someone had requested that Anjali dance. The crowd parted. Anjali stepped forward. A space opened up for her in front of our big-screen TV. Onlookers cheered as Anjali swung her hips from side to side and flicked her wrists like the head of a snake. It was impossible for us to know then what we know now: that life would consume her. That she would wake up one morning and decide to never dance again.

The next morning, I came back from my run and noticed a text message from a strange phone number. It was Anjali. She wanted to meet for brunch. She wore a thin white dress that highlighted the bronze tone of her skin. Her hair fell in loose waves. Over buttered rolls and mimosas, she confessed to me that she'd had a crush on me when we were young.

"I thought you were so cool with your cross-color jeans," she said. "But you must have thought I was a loser."

Had I missed all the signs? We ate thick waffles drizzled with syrup and crunchy fried chicken. I was surprised when Anjali paid the bill. She tore it from my hands. "This one's on me," she said. "After all, you're the one visiting."

Two days later, I took her to a Korean restaurant, where Anjali told me all about her life: her job at Walgreens, her applications to pharmacy school. Her parents wanted her to get married instead.

"Nothing I ever do will justify being single," she said. "I could be an astrophysicist and I'd still be single."

We talked about the parties we used to see each other at when we were young.

"I never wanted to go. I was always thinking about whatever football game or school dance I was missing," I said.

"I knew."

"You did?"

"You looked miserable."

She told me she had only moved out of her parents' house the month before. It was better this way. "Of course people talk," she said, spearing a piece of chicken and sliding it into her mouth. "But I need my privacy."

After a few drinks, I asked Anjali the question that had been lingering on my mind.

"Do you still talk to him? Your ex?"

"Vijay?" She laughed. "Oh god, no. He's dating some guy in Chicago. He's out and proud. You should see the two of them together: matching tank tops and all." She shook her head wistfully. "I must have been an idiot."

We developed a routine. In the afternoons I read and went for runs and waited for Anjali to get off work. Then we cooked dinner at my place or hers. She lived in an apartment with track lighting. She had a cat named Karma. The first time we made love she rolled over naked and strode into the kitchen, her bare ass dimpled and red.

"Where are you going?" I asked.

She returned with a camera. "Stop it," I said, when she started snapping pictures of my face.

"Why?" she asked, surprised. "You're beautiful."

I began seeing her in my dreams. I could close my eyes and

picture her exactly: her smoky eyes, her plum-toned lips, the small hard mole on her left cheek, the sun-bleached strands of orange in her hair.

She didn't dance anymore. The *lenghas* and bindis and blouses were packed away in a box, sealed with mothballs.

"I didn't like all those uncles staring at my breasts," she said.

Once, I asked her to dance for *me*—naked. She pinched me on my arm. "Those are boyfriend privileges."

"Am I not your boyfriend?"

She shrugged. "I don't know—are you?"

The question went unanswered: we both knew that I was.

Once, Anjali and I were at my parents' house watching a James Bond movie when the phone rang.

"It's my mother," I said.

"Is she scared you burned down the house?"

I nudged her with my foot; it was raining outside. Anjali wore my high school gym shirt over a pair of pink shorts.

"Answer it. I have to go now, anyway. I'm on the night shift."

She got up to leave when the phone went silent. "Wait." I pulled her into my embrace. "Stay."

She kissed me on the chin before getting up again. I followed her to the door. Just as she pulled out of the driveway, gliding onto the slick, mirrored road, my mother called again.

"Where were you?"

"Upstairs," I lied. "Why?"

"No reason." She relaxed. "I just haven't heard from you, that's all."

She whispered something to my father in the background, telling him to be quiet. Then she returned to the line.

"I talked to Sharmila Aunty today. She called to see how the baby was doing. She sent Rohan a gift. She said she saw you the other day, with Bharati Aunty's daughter, Anjali."

The way she mentioned Anjali's name made my neck feel hot.

"Where?" I asked.

"How should I know where? But listen: it is not a good match."

I walked into the kitchen and poured myself a drink. "We're just friends, Mom. I ran into her the other day. That's all."

"Friends," she said, slowly. "Friends—okay. Fine. But nothing more, *ha*?"

"Why?"

She clicked her tongue. "Are you asking me this? Didn't you hear what she did?"

"Of course I did. We all heard about the divorce. It's not like it was her fault."

"Her fault?" My mother laughed, cruelly. "What rubbish are you talking? Of course it was her fault. One hundred percent!"

Thunder cracked in the distance and punctuated my mother's words. She told me what had happened. "Three years ago, Anjali met Vijay at a bar. They started dating. The families met and everything went fine. Honestly, we were surprised. Vijay's parents are rich—very rich. What interest could they have in her? Anyway, Vijay and Anjali got married and that's when everything changed. Anjali went crazy. She accused Vijay of having an affair. She shouted at him in public. Once, she chased after him in the kitchen with a knife. She lied about things, too: where she was, what she was doing, whom she was with. Do you know—she was involved with a black man? *Hai bhagwan*. Vijay got tired of her lies and the marriage was over. But Anjali didn't stop. She showed up at his work one morning in a fit. She threatened to slash his tires. It wasn't until Vijay's parents called Bharati

Aunty to tell them what had happened that we found out the truth—*o mara baap!*

"She had problems," my mother whispered. "Mental problems. I am just thanking God that it was Vijay and not you."

My back was coated with sweat. Rohan needed a bath; my mother had to go.

"I thought he was gay."

"Who—Vijay?" she scoffed. "What nonsense. Who told you that?"

"No one."

She warned me not let Anjali into the house. "I don't want her there," she said. Then she hung up the phone.

That night, I lay awake in my bedroom and thought about what my mother had said. Why would Anjali lie? Our honesty, the ease with which we had revealed every layer of ourselves, was what I enjoyed most about us. I tossed and turned all night, picturing Anjali chasing me with a knife. My cell phone rang the next morning, but I couldn't pick up.

She sent a text: *Still sleeping?*

I ignored it and went for a run. Dr. Bernstein was pulling weeds from his yard. When I returned, jogging past brick houses with emerald lawns, there was a text message waiting for me on my phone.

Call me back.

She wanted to go swimming; the pool was open at her parents' motel. I packed my duffel bag with a bathing suit and flip-flops and drove over there. When I arrived, the clouds had cleared and Anjali was relaxing at the end of a turquoise-colored pool.

"It took you long enough."

She wore a two-piece bathing suit. Sunglasses shielded her eyes. Her legs shone like glazed chicken. I pulled up a lounge chair and lay down next to her.

"I used to come here every day as a child," she said, smearing sunscreen on her thighs.

Shards of light spiked off the pool's surface. In the distance, I could see a maid going into one of the motel rooms with a stack of white towels. "My thirteenth-birthday party was here. You were invited."

"I was?"

"You never came." She reached for my hand. "Not that I expected you to."

The coconut scent of her sunscreen made me hungry. I let her hand slip from mine.

"You had your wedding here, right?"

She stiffened. "Why do you ask?"

"No reason," I said. "I just remembered the invitation. I was invited."

"You were invited." She took a sip from her water bottle and screwed the cap back on. Then she got up and let her dark hair, coiled at her nape, fall neatly against her back. "Well, the whole world was invited," she said. "You weren't the only one. Now if you'll excuse me, I'm going for a swim." She dipped her toes into the pool before turning back around. "Unless you have any more *questions*."

She was in a foul mood after that. We didn't talk much as we dried and changed in one of the motel rooms and went for dinner at a Chinese restaurant nearby. Anjali slurped her noodles in silence.

"What were you doing this morning, anyway, that it took you so long to call me back?"

I looked up from my plate of orange chicken. "I was running."

"For five hours?"

"Yeah, and then I showered, and read, and had breakfast and lunch."

"It just seemed odd," Anjali said, twining noodles around her fork. "Usually you call me back right away."

I stared at her.

"I was busy."

"Busy." She wiped the grease from her fingers. "I see." Later, when we were leaving the restaurant, she brought it up again. "You were obviously on your phone. You liked a bunch of pictures on Instagram—who the hell is Shanaz?"

"Are you stalking me now?"

She wasn't amused. I must have struck a nerve, because she didn't speak to me the rest of the night. I dropped her home and she didn't invite me in. I didn't ask to be invited, either. The next morning she called me but I didn't call her back.

She called again. "Look, I'm sorry. I lost my head."

I didn't say anything.

"It's just that I really like you, Ankur. I wasn't expecting to—not so soon—but I do."

My mother's words reverberated through the back of my head. I shook them free. "I like you, too."

She was satisfied, suggesting we meet up that afternoon, for a picnic in the park. She would bring a bottle of wine. "There's something I've been meaning to tell you," she said.

And she hung up the phone.

That afternoon, I tried but failed to distract myself with a book. I watered the houseplants, made a sandwich in the kitchen. I skimmed through the pages of an old *Sports Illustrated* magazine.

I couldn't stand it anymore. I went into my parents' office and opened their file cabinet, which was filled with documents—SAT scores and tuition statements from college and beyond—and found a folder marked MISCELLANEOUS. Inside, stacks of greeting cards were bound together with a few expired passports and wedding invitations.

Anjali's was one of them.

The invitation smelled of mothballs, and was in the shape of a book. The cover was made of satin, flecked with rhinestones. Inside, loose, thin pages indicated the timings for various events: dinner parties and dances and the wedding itself, which took place on a Saturday in June. My mother had advised me not to attend it. "Don't even bother," she'd said. "God knows how it will be." I hadn't heard much about it, only that my parents hadn't stayed long. "The *chole* was off," they complained. "And the naan was like rubber."

I stared at the invitation now, noticing Anjali's name artfully linked with Vijay's. I logged on to Facebook and clicked on her page. I entered Vijay's name. There was nothing. I clicked on the search bar and entered it again: Vijay Desai. Out of a torrent of choices, only one of them could have been him: an accountant in Chicago. It was obvious. I remembered what Anjali had said, that Vijay was out and proud, but when I looked at his profile I saw nothing of the sort. His pictures—of himself in a crisp, black suit, playing baseball with friends, standing next to a woman who looked like a girlfriend or a wife—revealed nothing of his sexuality. His expression was stoic. Firm. The hairs on my neck stood on end. I closed the screen and picked up the loose pages of Anjali's wedding invitation and returned them to the cabinet. What purpose did my mother have in keeping it all these years? Perhaps she had been saving it to remind herself of the truth: that the world was a cruel and unpredictable place.

Anjali had asked me to meet her at 2 P.M. By two thirty, I still hadn't left, and she called. I didn't pick up. She called again. It would have been easy to invent something—an illness, an emergency, a sudden ache in my arms or my legs—but even that was too much. I kept hearing my mother's words ringing in the periphery, warning me. Anjali had wanted to tell me something that afternoon, but what? I thought about the last two months, images of her smiling face flickering through my mind. I put away my phone. I placed the ringer on mute. A week went by. The phone calls persisted. I was reminded of college, the way girls would call me for days before disappearing from sight. Anjali did the same. She sent a text one bright August morning: *I'm not sure what I did wrong, Ankur. Clearly you're not interested. I'll leave you alone now. Bye.*

And that was that.

It was easier than I had thought it would be. I turned off my cell phone and it was like Anjali had never existed. Still, I found her hair on my pillows and floors and in thick damp clumps in the drain. I went for runs every day. I read novels at night. I jogged past Dr. Bernstein's house and found Seth playing basketball outside.

"Hey, Seth," I said.

He passed me the ball. I shot it and missed.

"Weak, man. It's been a long time, but I see your basketball skills haven't changed."

I laughed. Seth had the same thick brown hair he'd had as a child, only this time it sprang up in wet curls.

"I kept seeing your father. I was hoping I'd run into you. I heard you're in a band."

"Just for fun," Seth said. "You should come see us play tonight. We'll have some beers."

He reached into his pocket and handed me a flyer. The bar was the same one where I had seen Anjali months ago. We talked about school and our lives and what we had been up to for the last decade. Then Seth had to get ready for rehearsal. "See you there?"

I told him he would.

At ten o'clock, I took a taxi to the bar. I entered just as Seth was taking the stage. It wasn't my scene: I was into hip-hop, mostly, Ghostface Killah and the Roots. Seth's band was a mix of alternative and punk. His skin glowed blue under the lights. His T-shirt clung to his chest. He shook his head from side to side and sweat danced off it like tiny sparks. The room was captivated, swaying left to right while reciting every lyric to every song. I had never seen that side of him before; at home, Seth was a cautionary tale my mother conjured up to keep my sister and me in line. *Is that what you want for yourselves,* she would say, her eyes smoldering, *to end up like Seth?* But in that moment, I envied him. His freedom. His will. It didn't matter where Seth was in life. It didn't matter who he'd become. On that particular night, and on that particular stage, he was whoever he wanted to be. I remembered the morning Dr. Bernstein told my father he had to switch his call for the weekend to visit Seth at college. It was an emergency. Seth was depressed.

"Depressed," my mother had said, laughing. "These whites are always *depressed*."

He didn't look depressed now. He was on fire, his eyes gleaming with the kind of bright intensity I had somehow lost in myself. Where did it go? The set was shorter than I had imagined. Seth wiped off with a towel; he made his way through the crowd.

"Seth," I said. "You were great up there."

He grinned. "Thanks, man. The sound was a little off, but what can you do?"

What can you do? My father had asked the same thing. I ordered Seth a beer and we caught up some more, trading stories from our past. Then Seth had to chat with his bandmates and I decided to call it a night, ordering another taxi home. The driver's name was Marcus. He was talkative. I lay my head against the seat cushion and listened to him, closing my eyes. It wasn't until we had parked in front of my house, under the gathering darkness, that Marcus noticed the car.

"Looks like you got company."

Through the rear glass of a Volvo, I could see the dark outline of Anjali's head, her engine running, headlights slicing the night.

I waved to Marcus and got into her car.

"What are you doing here?" I asked. She didn't answer me. "Hello?" I snapped my fingers in front of her face.

She was still gripping the steering wheel when she turned to face me, slowly.

"It's not true."

There was silence.

"I'm guessing you heard," she said. "I was racking my brain for days wondering what happened, why you disappeared. Then Sharmila Aunty walked up to me at the grocery store, and the way she mentioned your name made everything clear."

"Why did you lie to me?"

"I didn't."

"You did," I said. "You're crazy. You lied about everything. Everyone knows."

She looked as if I had just struck her across the face. I got out of the car. She followed me onto the lawn. My feet sank into soft, wet earth.

"Wait," she whispered.

I spun around. She was squinting at me.

"What do you think happens?" Her voice shook. "When a rich family finds out their only son is gay?"

I didn't answer her.

"Who do you think people believe? The girl?" Her voice trailed off. "Of course Vijay's parents denied everything. They still do. When they found out that, after six months of marriage, Vijay still hadn't touched me, they said it was my fault, that maybe I should lose some weight. The divorce was my idea, but Vijay's parents tried to intervene. When they couldn't, they made up some crazy story about me and told the whole world. And do you know what I learned?"

"What?" I said.

She glared at me.

"That if you're rich enough, people will believe anything you say—even the people you've known your whole life."

Tears fell from her eyes as she marched back to her car. I quickly followed her.

"Wait," I said, reaching for her arm. "I'm sorry. I didn't know."

"Right," she said.

Two weeks earlier, Anjali had tucked her legs between mine and asked me if I was her boyfriend; now she only stared at me, deciding I was not. I could have made some grand gesture—swept her up in my arms, distracted her with a kiss, professed my love for her in a song and dance, grazed her cheek like she was some heroine in a Bollywood film—but I didn't. We regarded each other silently, aware of the distance between us. Then Anjali got back into her car and the glare from her headlights, bright as laser beams, burned through my eyes.

The next morning I awoke with a headache. I went for a drive. I stopped by my old high school. I stared at the rows of small houses surrounding it, the cornfields just beyond, blazing under a flamingo sun. Had it been ten years? I could hardly imagine it. I dialed Anjali's number but she didn't pick up. I left her a voicemail but she didn't respond. I paced the parking lot, remembering the mornings when I had seen Anjali getting out of her father's car, wishing I had said hello.

That night, my parents called to tell me their plans had changed: they were returning early. Rohan was sleeping through the night. I cleaned the kitchen and emptied the bottles of scotch and replaced them with new ones from the store. I vacuumed the carpets and polished the floors. I removed every trace of Anjali from the house—a toothbrush, a hairpin, stray sequins from a strapless black dress—and tossed them into the trash. I had applied for a research fellowship at Northwestern and, upon being accepted, I moved to Chicago in the fall. I didn't see Anjali before I left. I tried calling her, but she didn't answer the phone. Soon, my parents reclaimed the house and there was no room for her, anyway.

In Chicago, I worked on residency applications while my roommates got drunk at bars. I thought about Anjali and wondered what she was doing, or if she was still thinking about me. Girls slept over and I smelled the scent of her perfume. A memory of something she had once said would pop into my mind. For weeks I tried finding her on Facebook but couldn't; her account was disabled. Finally, I sent her a text: *Can we talk?* She was quick with her reply: *I don't think that's a very good idea, Ankur.* And that was the end. She disappeared from my thoughts, the way a T-shirt's color, vibrant and new, disappears in the wash. It wasn't until a year later, when I had matched into an Internal Medicine program in Riverside, California, and the black mark of my failure had been cleanly erased, that my mother called with the news.

"You won't believe. You won't believe what I just heard. Do you remember Bharati Aunty's daughter—Anjali?"

My heart stopped.

"Yeah?"

"She's getting married."

I dropped my headphones onto the counter; I had just come from a run. Sweat poured down my back and seeped into the waistband of my shorts.

"She met a man online," my mother said. "An engineer. He works for Boeing. He is divorced. Do you know what else?"

I waited for her to continue.

"No one is invited to the wedding. Not a single person. Out of the whole entire Indian community—not one."

I smiled. My mother went on to criticize Anjali's parents for isolating themselves from the Indian community, for turning their backs on everyone who had turned their backs on them. But I no longer listened. I closed my eyes and imagined the peach shimmer of Anjali's *lengha,* fanned out at her waist. I saw the flare of her hips. I remembered that night in my parents' living room when I was twelve years old. In my recollection, Anjali had spun around the room like a tornado, her blouse flashing, her lips glinting. Spinning and spinning. Until she was gone. ♦

radha, krishna

You have no idea what it was like for me, the morning you left. I drove by your house as you were packing your car. I was parked on your street. Of course you didn't see me. You wore a green T-shirt and your hair, so black it shone blue, was tucked under a hat. After you hugged your parents good-bye, you followed a tree-lined path toward the highway. What a privilege it must have been, to drive through their neighborhood, to see the world through their eyes, to live a life of certainty and assurance when so few things are certain or assured.

I still remember that last night on your driveway, when you looked at me and saw nothing. Perhaps you saw right through me, into one of the houses beyond. What was it like to grow up in a house like that? Did your ego swell like a grain of rice? Did you enjoy the look of hunger in my parents' eyes? I would never know. I grew up in a small apartment above my parents' motel, with sounds of cars on the highway. I stared out my window and saw endless rows of corn. I cowered when white men shouted at my father in the lobby: *Speak English!* I danced in my bedroom to Bollywood songs, thinking of you.

If you open your high school yearbook, you will find my picture next to yours. Our first names are similar. Our last names are the same. Because of this, everyone had assumed you were my brother. I was embarrassed to tell them the truth: that I was in love with you. Of course you didn't know it at the time. What you knew instead was that I was the girl your parents forced you to say hi to at dinner parties you were reluctant to attend.

Your parents knew mine only vaguely. Your father was a doctor. My father owned a motel. Your father dressed in business suits—mine, in old T-shirts. Your mother was elegant, with jewels glistening at her throat. My mother wore the same saris for years. I saw the way your mother slit her eyes whenever I walked by. Do you know what it's like, to make a woman's face go sour? Probably you don't. Women look at you only sweetly.

We'd met in grade school, but it was at a rec center one evening, on a cold autumn night, that I first began to notice you. I was thirteen at the time, and my breasts were budding. It was Navratri, the nine-day festival in which we danced around an altar, decorated with marigold petals. That was how I had explained it to my best friend in high school, Sarah. Sarah was with me that night, in a *ghagra choli*. I had wanted to give her a new one but my mother had refused.

"What difference does it make?" she'd said. "Old or new, what does Sarah care?"

You wore a baseball cap and you smelled like cologne. Your Air Jordans were unlaced, your flannel shirt untucked. Your carelessness was careful, your confidence, a con. I saw right through you. Maybe you knew, because when I said hello to you, you pretended not to hear it. You strode around the room instead, looking bored. I danced with my friends and ate puris on the floor and gossiped about who had been drinking or whose breasts had been touched. You were nowhere to be found. I longed to be in your world. At school, your friends were mostly white boys and black boys who listened to Bone Thugs-N-Harmony. I assumed you were ashamed of me. I was evidence of the world you shrugged off each morning before you entered the room.

Of course you denied all of this in your bedroom the summer you came back into my life. We were older then. You traced my eyelids with your finger, and pinched the fat on my thighs, and flicked your tongue against my neck. You said I was beautiful. What was beautiful was your reflection in my eyes. Did you think I didn't notice? The way you stood a few inches taller when showing me your parents' brick house, or their brand-new sedan, with its thick, perforated leather? You saw only my devotion to you, like Radha's devotion to Krishna, like Lakshmi's devotion to Vishnu, like my mother's devotion to my father, like the ocean's devotion to the moon. I remember my mother showing me pictures of Lord Krishna as a child, with his soft navy skin. He was surrounded by women, hundreds of them, some old enough to be his mother, all with the same doleful look in their eyes. I asked my mother what they were doing there and she said simply that they were in love. A thousand women: all vying for the attention of a man.

I swore I would never become one of those women, so I married a man who is nothing like you. His name is Jacob. He's an engineer. Brown fuzz covers his arms and his legs. His eyes, green pools the shade of summer, are flecked with gold. How can it be? That a white man could have so many colors? We'd met online. By that point, after the disaster of my first marriage, my parents were relieved; brown men had taken issue with the fact that I was divorced. White men had not. What mattered was that Jacob was successful. He was kind. According to my mother, he was like Vishnu—he restored order to my world.

Through Jacob, I was able to escape the rumors and gossip and former prison of my childhood town. Even my parents were spared, having successfully raised a daughter in a country that was not their own. The pictures I sent them—of Jacob's silver Lexus, of my brand-new Jeep, of our chocolate-colored house in Michigan with skylights and stone floors—were proof that they had fulfilled their duty, despite what anyone else said. Jacob accepted a position as the dean of a college engineering program. I finished my degree in pharmacy. Between the two of us, we built a life for ourselves that most people would envy. Our kids, twin girls with skin that glowed like metal and eyes so pale people wondered if they were real, were the crowning achievement of my parents' lives. When we closed on our house, they threw a party and invited some of the Indian families from our hometown to see it. I hesitated at first, remembering what they had said about us, reminding her that we had never been close, but my mother insisted, and I could sense in her tone a kind of desperation. By that point, I had risen in the community's esteem. All those years my mother had pretended to be comfortable on the outskirts of the Indian community, but in that moment, I knew: she wanted a way back in. So I let her host a puja in my honor, and bury a coconut in our backyard, and invite a priest over to chant above a small flame. He blessed the property, our marriage, our lives. Jacob and I linked hands and accepted gifts and showed off the spectacular central staircase and marble master bath.

I still don't know if I love him. I see his face in the mornings and feel at ease. I hear his keys in the lock and wait for him to enter. I cook him chicken curry and watch him clean his plate. I do the things I watched my mother do, things I swore I would never do when I was sixteen. I pack lunches and wash trousers and stand on my feet for twelve hours a day, and sometimes, late at night, after scrubbing Play-Doh off the kitchen counter, I wonder if it was all worth it. The desperation I had once felt, the urgency even, is now gone. At the time, Jacob had seemed like my only option—it is clear to me, now, that he was simply a choice.

I had assumed you and I would never see each other again, and for a while, I was right. Jacob and I lived in Michigan. You had moved to California. The thread that had once bound us was severed, too frayed for repair. I had convinced myself that it was never meant to be, that we were star-crossed lovers, but when I saw you that weekend at Nishali and Mehul's wedding, in the bright lobby of a Marriott hotel, I began to wonder, for a moment, if I had been wrong.

The wedding was my parents' idea. They had wanted me to reconnect with the people from my past. I suspect the real reason was to show me off; the daughter who once had nothing, now had everything. My mother was always asking me to send her pictures of Jacob and the girls and the house and the cars, and the little things, too, like a shrimp risotto we had once ordered at a restaurant. I understood, then, that those pictures were not meant for my parents' benefit but for their friends', that my presence at Nishali's wedding, my postmarital glow, was a form of redemption.

Your parents were in Europe for the summer; your sister was saddled with kids. Because of this, it was you who came in their place. By then, the girls were in kindergarten and Jacob was golfing and no one was inspired enough to board a plane to Chicago, for the wedding of a person they barely knew. So I came without them. I did not expect to see you at all, but then I remembered that Nishali—my childhood friend—was your cousin; the groom, your classmate in med school. In many ways you had more of a reason to be there than I did.

It was the night before the wedding, two hours before the *sangeet,* and I had just flown in. Women and children lounged on sofas in the lobby. Husbands checked into the rooms. The windows were tall and streaky. The floors, speckled tiles that squeaked loudly underfoot, were polished bright. I had picked up my room key and was waiting for my mother to drop by with some jewelry when you walked through the doors. You wore a black blazer, distressed jeans. Your hair was slicked back. A piece of luggage trailed your feet. It looked expensive. Everything about you did.

A few uncles and aunties recognized you immediately and began commenting on your weight. It was then that I noticed it. Your face was angular, your arms and legs lean; the swell of your stomach, once prominent but firm, had deflated. You laughed it off and made a joke about the pressure of living in California, and the matter was resolved. Your voice carried across the lobby and landed sharply in my chest, awakening inside of me what I'd once thought was dead. Panicked, I escaped into the elevator and closed my eyes. I had not expected to feel this way at all.

Just as I was arranging my perfumes and lipsticks and jewelry on the bathroom counter, the phone rang, and, foolishly, I hoped it was you. Perhaps you had seen me, and had asked the hotel receptionist for my room number. I remembered all those evenings when you had called to apologize and I had never answered, not because I didn't love you, but because it was obvious that you could never love me. I made my way to the telephone and glanced out the window, which overlooked the sun-drenched lobby, the tropical plants, wedding guests milling around a large fountain. I answered the phone, waiting to hear your voice again.

How stupid of me.

"Make it in okay?" Jacob said.

"Yes."

"How is it so far?"

"It's strange." I flicked on the TV. A newscaster's somber face appeared, reporting a shooting. "I don't recognize anyone yet. I haven't seen Nishali. I'm supposed to go by her room to pick up my bridesmaid outfit."

"I'm sorry we didn't come."

"Don't be. Now I can relax with a glass of wine."

"Of course you can," Jacob said, laughing. "This is a dream come true for you."

"How are the girls?"

"Rumi wants you to bring her a present. Simran is watching *Moana* for the third time. All in all, we're wonderful."

"Great. I miss them—and you."

"We miss you, too."

I stared at the flashing alarm clock between two quilted beds, realizing it was time to get ready.

"I should go," I said. "This outfit is complicated, and I can barely remember how to put it on."

"Feel free to drunk-dial me."

I smiled as I hung up the phone, suddenly craving a drink. It had been so long since I had been in a quiet room alone. I found a bottle of white wine in the minibar and poured myself a glass. The woman was still reporting about the shooting. The voices still rose from the lobby. My suitcase was unpacked and pink and orange fabrics spilled out from it like a dragon's tongue. I closed my eyes and thought of you.

Downstairs, wedding guests sparkled in brilliant colors: crimson and lilac and silver and gold. You were nowhere to be found. I met up with a few girls from the bridal party and walked into the banquet hall. They sipped cocktails and talked about how drunk they'd been at the bachelorette party, which had taken place in Miami. I had not been there, and after a while, they grew tired of my silence, walking away from me. I ordered a drink at the bar. I stood around for a bit, smiling and waving to people from afar, when I noticed your face.

"Anything else?" the bartender asked, pouring me my wine.

You wore a white kurta with gold threading and pointed, elflike shoes. I had not expected you to wear such a thing. You, who poked fun at everything Indian, who refused to watch Bollywood films, who swore you would never have an Indian wedding because they were a waste of money and time. Your hair was gelled back. You had shaved. The effect was startling: the sudden sharpness of your jaw, the hollowness of your cheeks, the slim lines of your neck, more visible now. You looked boyishly handsome, but there was wisdom in your eyes, as if you had seen things I would never know about, things I longed to understand. I had heard that you were still single. The few times my mother mentioned your name were in reference to this fact, that your parents were worried: you were thirty-five and still a bachelor. I defended you, saying it was none of their business, that marriage wasn't for everyone, that sometimes you think you know what you want and the universe has a way of telling you otherwise.

It would have been the perfect time to greet you, but my parents arrived, whisking me away toward their friends. My mother was clasping the hand of another woman, and her solicitude, the sparkle in her eyes when she introduced us, made me want to slap her.

"Anjali, look at you now," the woman said. "So well settled."

Well settled. The image that came to mind was that of a very fat bird, guarding its nest.

"And the girls," she said. "*Chal chal.* Let us see. Where are the pictures?"

I pulled out my phone, scrolling through the pictures, answering her questions about their favorite colors, their favorite foods. She looked at me sharply.

"Do they love their Indian? Or do they love their burger and fries?"

"Indian, of course," my mother said. "Rumi adores my *kichuri*."

"Kya baat!"

Had you been there, I would have rolled my eyes and told you how stupid this all was. The girls were half Indian: what did she expect? Just the other day, Rumi had declared *kichuri* inedible. But instead I smiled, reinforcing my mother's lie. We stood at a table and ate puffed snacks with green chutney, fat cubes of paneer. People began to dance, and through the swish of flowing fabrics—gold, pink, yellow, blue—I saw your face.

Just as I approached you, you turned around. Your back was facing me, so close that I could feel the heat from your skin. White strands threaded your lush black hair. Had they always been there? I longed to touch them, but I was too slow, and soon you were swept up into the crowd, raising your arms. I had never seen you dance before. You were always so stoic during those parties at your parents' house, as if you were waiting for all of us to leave, waiting to return to your room, waiting for the evening to be over so you could no longer pretend. Were you pretending that summer, when you told me you wished you had noticed me sooner, that you would do anything in your power to make up for lost time?

That night, I met Nishali and the other bridesmaids in the hotel lobby for drinks. She looked beautiful, with jewels crusting her wrists and her neck. We talked about dating and marriage and where we wanted to end up in ten years. Then she mentioned your name.

"He looks good—different, but good."

"He's lost weight."

"That's what it was. I couldn't figure it out at first." She smiled. "Do you still talk to him?"

"Does anyone?"

"I figured if anyone did it would be you."

I told her the truth: that I hadn't seen or heard from you in years, and that you were living in California. She nodded, as if she had expected this. After a while, Nishali ordered a round of shots for everyone and proposed a toast. "Photographs are at eight A.M.," she said, before escaping to her room. I hung around for a bit, making small talk with the girls, showing them pictures of Rumi and Simran, answering their questions about marriage and sex, before I, too, retired to my room.

It was in the hallway of my floor, past the elevators and vending machines and a corridor stocked with an ice dispenser that hummed noisily into the night, that I saw you—talking to a girl. You had changed, into a black button-down shirt over jeans. The sleeves were rolled up and the hair on your arms was thick. The girl, in a lime-green sari, was touching her hair in a way that revealed her interest in you. I burned with envy. I was reminded of high school, when girls had looked at you from afar and the gleam in their eyes, sharp as kitchen blades, had cut through my skin. But you were bored. You nodded your head, and shifted your feet, and stared at the gold dial on your watch, and laughed at her jokes in a perfunctory way. And I was relieved. Me, a woman who was married with two girls, relieved that the man I hadn't seen for years was uninterested in a girl I scarcely knew. And that's when you saw me.

"Anjali?"

It was your suggestion that we go to my room. Your room was two floors above. The girl, a young woman your mother had wanted you to meet, was the daughter of family friends. You wished her good night in a way that let her know you were not interested in her. Then you stared at me.

"I haven't seen you in ages. You look great."

My hands shook as I slipped the key card into the door and kicked aside the towels and closed the curtains so that no one would see us, even though all you wanted to do was chat. Still, it felt illicit. You sat on one of the beds, bouncing lightly against the comforter, and I sat on the chair opposite, so there would be no confusion.

"Thanks," I said. "I would say the same, except there's less of you now."

You laughed. "Everyone keeps telling me to eat. It's called the L.A. diet: kale salads and weed."

"You never needed a diet."

"Everyone needs a diet."

"God—you really are a Californian."

Dimples formed in the hollows of your cheeks. You turned your head, feigning interest in the cardboard pyramid of TV channels on the nightstand. Your eyes flicked past the minibar, suggesting a drink.

"Help yourself."

"Won't you join me?"

"I have to be up in five hours," I said, glancing at the alarm clock. But you poured me a drink anyway, and I accepted it, eager to let the warm buzz embrace me again. You started unbuttoning your shirt, and my heart raced, but then you stopped at the collarbone. I could see the dark hair on your chest.

For a while it was simple. We told each other everything we had wanted to know: my marriage, your fellowship, my move to Michigan, your practice in Orange County, my husband and children and career, your bachelorhood. We had one drink and then another. At some point I floated over to the bed opposite yours, and we sat facing each other, our eyes reflecting the square light of the lamp.

"So tell me—what was so wrong with that girl in the hallway?"

"She's twenty-five." You laughed. "I can't date someone who's never listened to Biggie Smalls."

"And in California? No one?"

"No one special."

Was I special? I wanted to know. But I would never ask. I could never bring myself to hear the answer.

Instead I asked you questions about your family—your father's retirement, your sister's three kids, the lavish party your parents had thrown for their fortieth wedding anniversary. We talked about the people from our hometown with whom both of us had lost touch. There were things you knew about me that my husband would never know, things I would never have to explain to you. It was easy in a way it hadn't been with anyone else.

At one point, you got up to pour yourself a drink, and instead of returning to the bed opposite mine, you sat right next to me. I could smell the cologne on your shirt. You turned to look at me and your breath was warm against my face. You said something, I can't even remember it now, but whatever it was loosened me. Did your lips purse to meet mine? Did you lean in for a kiss? I will never know. Just then, my phone rang, and it was Jacob. I had forgotten to check in.

"It might be the girls," I said, at which you stood up and placed your hands around your neck.

"I should go."

"Wait—stay."

"It's late."

"This will only take a second."

You smiled at me and shook your head, as if you knew that it wouldn't. Then you walked out of the room. Part of me wanted to go with you, to convince you to stay, but by then I was already answering, wishing I hadn't.

The next morning, I awoke in a daze. I showered and changed into the white sari Nishali had provided each of us the night before. At breakfast, I ate *gathiya* with pickled chilies. I searched the room for you, but you were not there. Probably you were still sleeping. My parents introduced me to more friends and relatives, and soon the *baraat* began, in which we danced outside the hotel lobby. Aunties and uncles circled a horse-drawn carriage. The groom, decked in a pink turban, began to dance, flanked by groomsmen. You were not one of them. I had assumed you and Mehul were close. Obviously you were not. The drums grew louder and louder, the groomsmen jumping up and down, scraping the sky with their fingers. Women linked hands and spun in circles, their mirrored saris reflecting sequins of light. It wasn't until the procession had moved back into the lobby that I saw you, drinking a coffee in your suit.

"Save me a seat?"

I nodded, and the intimacy of your smile, the way no one seemed to notice, sent a chill down my spine. You arrived just in time, before the lights went dim and the double doors opened and the bride floated out to a gasping applause. Her *chunari* glittered like rubies. Her arms were shackled in gold. She looked like a bedazzled prisoner.

"Why is she walking like that?" you said, snickering. "Does she have to take a shit?"

I laughed so loud an entire row of aunties turned to shush me. You pinched me on my arm. I flicked you on your ear. In the entire banquet facility, we were the only two people touching.

Later, when the bride and groom were preparing to walk around a fire, garlands hanging from their necks, you turned your head and asked, "Was your wedding like this?"

I glanced at you.

"Oh, shit," you said, realizing your mistake. "I forgot."

"It's okay. Jacob and I didn't have a wedding. We had a court ceremony. And don't even ask about the first one."

We didn't talk for a while, focusing on the ceremony. At one point, you left the room altogether and returned with a glass of water. You reached into your back pocket and took out a white pill.

"What's that?" I asked.

"A party favor."

"You really have changed."

You shrugged. "I have to entertain myself somehow."

After the ceremony, we skipped lunch and went to a park. It felt daring, slipping away like that, just the two of us. The sun was high and the sky was the color of a peacock's breast.

"I should go—Nishali will be pissed."

"Do you even care?"

You reached for my hand and I let you hold it. I never knew a simple act could feel so tremendous, like we were moving a mountain together, striking a fire. I could tell you felt it, too. We were silent for a while, staring out at the pond and the rows of benches surrounding it and the small family of ducks with their iridescent feathers. It felt surreal being there with you, just like it had that summer.

I would have let you kiss me then, but within moments a family from the wedding came to join us.

"We've been spotted."

"We could go to the room," I said.

You shook your head. "I have to meet another girl. My parents set it up. She lives thirty minutes from here."

My heart fell, and you must have sensed this because you said, "I guess I could cancel."

"No, don't. We'll meet at the reception."

"Before. I'll stop by your room."

"Okay then."

And for a moment I actually believed that you would.

By five thirty, you still hadn't arrived, and I got ready in my room, pinning the pleats of a black sari to my blouse. One of the bridesmaids found me and invited me to have drinks with her at the bar, so I followed her with a glass of white wine. Sitar music strummed from the speakers. Ice sculptures melted over plates. A group of men were huddled in a corner, drinking whiskey and beer. I had assumed you would be with them. You were not. I stared at my phone, sending a text message to Jacob, telling him I missed him, missing you instead. Did you still have my phone number? I hadn't asked. Before long the cocktail hour ended and guests filtered into the next room, which sparkled like a crushed gem.

"Anjali," one of the bridesmaids said, "you're sitting with us."

I slipped into a rattan chair and stared at the backlit walls, which glowed purple and pink. The tables were covered in black lace. The glasses were fluted and crystal. My wedding was nothing like this. My wedding had only eight guests: Jacob's family and mine. I had seen the way my mother eyed Nishali at the ceremony. I had felt her hunger in the pit of my own gut.

After the speeches and dances and dinner, the reception was over. I had spent the majority of my time at the table, nursing my wine. My parents went to sleep early. The bridesmaids were drunk. According to one of them, there was an after-party in a suite stocked with pizza and booze. I declined her invitation, and she didn't push me to reconsider. You were nowhere to be found. Not among the clusters of men drinking Johnnie Walker. Not by the dessert table with its chocolate fondue. Not on the dance floor full of teenagers doing the Nae Nae. Not even outside, by the park we had visited, getting a breath of fresh air. You had not given me your room number, and so, at one thirty, after most of the guests had cleared, only a few lingering on sofas and chairs, I approached the front desk and asked if they might have it.

"His name is Ankur Patel. I haven't seen him all day. I'm a little worried."

"Are you related?" the desk clerk, a large woman with red cheeks and snowy white hair, wanted to know.

I hesitated, remembering how in high school everyone had assumed you were my brother.

"Patel," I said, pulling out my ID. "See?"

She laughed. "Oh, honey. This hotel is full of Patels. You're going to have to be more specific than that."

I smiled, stepping away.

"I wish I could help," she called after me.

I walked past the lobby and into an open elevator. I could hear the sound of laughter above. I considered going to the party—maybe you were there—but changed my mind. My flight was before noon. I had already said good-bye to my parents—they were skipping breakfast the next morning so they could head back to the motel. Somehow, the idea of this made me sad, and I began to cry. Tears slid past my cheeks and my lips. I looked at my phone and realized that Jacob had called moments earlier, and this made me cry even harder. I pictured him in his Notre Dame T-shirt, cleaning up after the girls. They would be sound asleep in their Princess Jasmine beds. By the time I reached my hallway, I had pulled myself together, fishing out the hotel key from my purse and sliding it through the lock. The room was chilly and quiet, just as I had left it.

Only this time you were there.

"What took you so long?"

You wore the same suit you had worn that morning, but your jacket was slung over a chair, your shirt unbuttoned. The sight of you lifted me like a leaf in a breeze. You were lying on my bed, with your arms tucked behind your head as if it had been your room and not mine. I had always liked that about you, the way you could inhabit any space as if it belonged to you first.

"You missed the reception. You're a terrible wedding guest."

"I was hoping we could skip it," you said. "I got back pretty late. By the time I came by the room you were already downstairs."

"How did you even get in? I don't remember giving you a key."

You winked at me. "I have my ways."

"No, really," I said. "This is scary. What if you had been someone else?"

"Don't worry about it."

I searched the room for a sign of forced entry. There was nothing. I glanced back at the TV. An advertisement for cough medicine flashed across the screen.

"Now what?" I said.

It was easier this time, to have your skin against mine, your lips against mine, your fingers tracing my back, unbuttoning my blouse. You were hungry for my body, kissing and groping and sucking, and I fed you every piece. Did you remember what it was like, to have me this way? I did. I remembered the smell of your hair and the taste of your skin. I remembered the cold tickle of your fingers on my thighs. I remembered the noises you made when I did something you liked. It was a peculiar sound, so unlike your usual voice. I should have felt guilty. I should have felt ashamed. I felt everything but. I ran my fingers over you and felt the newness of your body, rigid and firm. Your waistline was narrow, your stomach defined. Your arms were like rubber, ropey and weak. After it was over, you told me your date had been a disaster.

"She was twice the size of her photograph," you said.

I pinched you on your arm, relieved. How foolish of me.

The next morning, you woke up early and showered in my bathroom and combed your hair back in front of the mirror, enveloped in steam. You kissed me and asked if we would ever see each other again. I laughed at this and told you we would. There were other weddings, other weekends to be shared. It was just the beginning. You went quiet, and I wondered what you were thinking. I packed my suitcase while you watched me, a smile on your face. How could it be? That a smile could hide such secrets?

We went to the park one last time, and sat on a bench overlooking the pond, and you picked up a small stone and tried to skip it, missing the water. The sun was warm against my skin.

"Weddings are weird," you said. "All that pomp and circumstance, all that drama, and for what? Do people even remember them?"

"No," I said, unable to hide the bitterness in my voice. "But I'm guessing one day you'll find out."

You didn't say anything. Then you put your hand over mine and said, very softly, "I'm not getting married, " and I glanced at my wristwatch and realized it was time to leave.

You insisted on driving me to the airport—you had rented a car—so we slipped out of the hotel without saying good-bye to anyone. During the drive, you were silent, and I was fighting back tears. Jacob was waiting for me. But I could only think of you.

When we pulled up alongside the terminal you switched off the car.

"I'm sorry."

"About last night?" I gathered my things. "So you were a little late; it happens. At least we got to see each other."

"Not that." You shook your head. A plane descended over our heads and cast a shadow over your face. "I'm sorry about everything else. The way I treated you, when we were young, and after—for letting you go."

I put my hand on your arm. "Stop."

But you didn't. Cars rushed by and an attendant came over to tell you to move, but you only stared at him. "To be honest—and this might sound weird—but I was a little jealous of you back then. We all were. You had this aura about you. It's like you were somewhere else. You were there, but you were somewhere else. I never had that for myself."

I stared at you, uncomprehending. We were quiet for a while. Then you got out of the car and helped me with my luggage and when I looked into your eyes, I knew: something was wrong.

That was the last time we saw each other. I still remember the way you waited until I had walked past the sliding glass doors before getting back into your car, the heat from your embrace still warming my skin. It was impossible to talk after that. I returned to my world, and you returned to yours. Jacob picked me up with the girls, and I kissed each one of them on their heads. My life resumed its course: play dates and meetings and dinner parties with friends, day trips to a museum or a park. For months, I thought of you, our fated weekend returning to me like a dream, but then something would happen—a cut that needed tending, a fight between the kids, a large bill in the mail—and you would be plucked from my thoughts, the way a blade of grass, rooted to the earth, is plucked by a child. I didn't stop to wonder where you were, or what you were doing. I didn't do any of this until eight months later, on a cold winter morning, when I was standing alone in the kitchen and the phone suddenly rang. I had assumed it would be Jacob, calling to talk to me from work, or one of the teachers at school, calling to talk about the girls, but instead it was my mother, calling to talk about *you*.

"Something has happened."

I know what it's like: to have people say things about you that aren't true. I had heard the rumors about myself. You will never know what I heard about you. According to some people, you had developed a rare form of cancer. Others said it was something more insidious, and shameful. Still others said you were on drugs, that you had done it to yourself. You were a doctor. How could you not have known? The question I ask myself is: How could I? You said you were on a diet and I believed you. I turned my head when you popped that white pill. I laughed at you when you asked if we would see each other again. I cursed you in my head when you didn't show up to my room. I didn't think to ask what you had been doing all that time. I didn't want to know. It is clear to me, now, that you were ill.

Is that why you never married? For weeks after it happened, people would ask this same thing, as if the greatest tragedy of all was that you had left no one behind. Your parents said it was pneumonia, that you had suffered complications. But your obituary was left vague; your family was tight-lipped. There were more questions than answers, questions no one had the courage to ask.

A picture ran next to the small article about you in my parents' local newspaper; it was your high school yearbook photo. In it, you wore a gold earring in your left ear; your hair was buzzed short. How strange that you should be remembered that way. For weeks after hearing the news, I walked around like a ghost, as if I had left my own body in the way you had left yours. I couldn't sleep, or eat. I never made it to your funeral, either. Your parents didn't want anyone there. Your mother was too distraught. She called my mother one morning to apologize. She said finally she knew—she knew what it was like to have people talk about her child.

On the way to the airport that morning, I had asked you again. "How did you get into my hotel room?"

You smiled.

"I had a key."

"Did you steal it?"

"No."

"Did I give to you?"

"No."

"Then how?"

You turned your head and laughed. "I got it from the front desk."

"But that's impossible," I said. "They wouldn't even give me your room number."

"I have my ways."

"Tell me—how?"

And you did.

"I told them you were my wife."

I never told you this, but that summer, before you left, I had dreamt of marrying you. I remembered my mother showing me pictures of Lord Krishna when I was a child. I remembered the hordes of women that surrounded him. Only one of them had captured his heart, a young woman named Radha. According to my mother, they never married, but their love for each other remained, long after Krishna had died, immortalized in the small pictures that lined our apartment walls. Like you, my mother is long gone now, and the girls are in college, but the pictures remain, and sometimes, when I look at them, I can still see your face. ♦

Acknowledgments

I'm very grateful to my agent, Jenni Ferrari-Adler, for plucking me out of the slush pile and giving me a chance, for her insight, her dedication, and for making my dream come true. This book would not be what it is without the help of my brilliant editor, Caroline Bleeke, whose commitment, wisdom, and enthusiasm made the long hours worth it—whenever I was lost, she helped show me the way. To Amy Einhorn and the rest of the team at Flatiron Books, thank you for this wonderful opportunity.

A writer is nothing without faithful readers. To the editors who gave early versions of these stories a home: thank you. Without journals like yours, writers like me would not dare to dream. To my television champions at WME, Lauren Szurgot and Flora Hackett, thank you for reading this book and encouraging me to try my hand at something new. You saw something in me before I even did, and for that I'm grateful.

To my friends both near and far, past and present, the ones I've lost touch with, the ones I speak to every day, thank you for sharing your time with me, your laughter, your tears. I hope, in this book, you have found something to love.

To my family, my sister, for being a champion and a friend, and my parents, for being there from the beginning, when I needed you the most, even when I didn't need you at all. You are the reason I am what I am. I hope I make you proud.

And finally, to the scared little boy who was afraid to be himself: be afraid no longer. This book is for you. Everything that follows is for both of us.